"I've died and gone to heaven."

The pool looked so lovely, so inviting. Miranda found an inner tube and threw it in, then dove off the board, loving that first icy shock of water against her skin. She swam several laps, then rested awhile at the edge. Nymphs and sprites and goddesses regarded her benignly from all around, but other than that, the terrace was deserted. Someone had left a pair of sunglasses lying on the side, and she grabbed them before swimming off again. Plunging underwater, she resurfaced inside the inner tube and lay back upon it, her head resting on the rim, her hair flowing out in the water, the sun warm and gentle on her face.

Heaven, she thought delightedly.

The water made little lapping sounds around her head. Lulling sounds. Lulling her into a light, lazy sleep . . .

There was no warning.

Just a slight tremor as the statue began to tip.

And then the crash—

The swift downward plunge as she felt herself being pushed to the very bottom of the pool.

The water rushing full force into her lungs . . .

Books by Richie Tankersley Cusick

Buffy the Vampire Slayer
  (a novelization based on a screenplay by Joss Whedon)
The Drifter
Fatal Secrets
Help Wanted
The Locker
The Mall
Overdue
Silent Stalker
Someone at the Door
Starstruck
Summer of Secrets
Vampire

Available from ARCHWAY Paperbacks

For orders other than by individual consumers, Pocket Books grants a discount on the purchase of **10 or more** copies of single titles for special markets or premium use. For further details, please write to the Vice-President of Special Markets, Pocket Books, 1633 Broadway, New York, NY 10019-6785, 8th Floor.

For information on how individual consumers can place orders, please write to Mail Order Department, Simon & Schuster Inc., 200 Old Tappan Road, Old Tappan, NJ 07675.

RICHIE TANKERSLEY CUSICK

Starstruck

AN ARCHWAY PAPERBACK
Published by POCKET BOOKS
New York London Toronto Sydney Tokyo Singapore

The sale of this book without its cover is unauthorized. If you purchased this book without a cover, you should be aware that it was reported to the publisher as "unsold and destroyed." Neither the author nor the publisher has received payment for the sale of this "stripped book."

This book is a work of fiction. Names, characters, places and incidents are products of the author's imagination or are used fictitiously. Any resemblance to actual events or locales or persons, living or dead, is entirely coincidental.

AN ARCHWAY PAPERBACK *Original*

An Archway Paperback published by
POCKET BOOKS, a division of Simon & Schuster Inc.
1230 Avenue of the Americas, New York, NY 10020

Copyright © 1996 by Richie Tankersley Cusick

All rights reserved, including the right to reproduce this book or portions thereof in any form whatsoever. For information address Pocket Books, 1230 Avenue of the Americas, New York, NY 10020

ISBN: 0-671-55104-3

First Archway Paperback printing November 1996

10 9 8 7 6 5 4 3 2 1

An ARCHWAY PAPERBACK and colophon are registered trademarks of Simon & Schuster Inc.

Cover art by Phil Schramm

Printed in the U.S.A.

IL: 7+

to Robert Cosgrove,
for your honesty, integrity,
and friendship

Starstruck

1

The young woman slipped to the edge of the roof. Her hands grabbed frantically for a hold, and her scream echoed on and on through the rainy night.

"Oh, God," Miranda whispered. "She's really going to fall!"

The woman dangled high above the wet, busy streets. Her face was a mask of horror and stunned resignation as she prepared to plunge to her death.

"She's going to die!" Miranda gasped.

"Oh, be quiet," her younger sister, Lynn, muttered. "It's only a stupid movie. And you've already seen it ten times—you act like you don't know how it's gonna end."

"*You* be quiet!" Miranda threw back at her, scooting to the edge of the couch. "Here's the best part!"

In the next second the TV screen filled with the handsome, chiseled face of the hero, his dark hair blown wildly by the wind, his dark eyes narrowed in total concentration.

His hand grasped the woman's wrist.

As she sobbed and struggled, he slowly began to pull her upward.

"Big surprise," Lynn grumbled. "Byron Slater saves the day one more time."

Miranda sighed. "I wish he'd save *my* day."

"Yeah, you and every other female in the universe. That woman sort of looks like you, doesn't she? Too bad *you* can't fall off some roof."

"What do you mean, she looks like me? Just because she has blond hair? You think every actress with blond hair looks like me."

"No, only the really ugly ones. Can we please put something *else* in now? Before Mom and Dad get home and make me start studying?"

"No. I have to watch the whole thing."

"You mean the part at the end where he kisses the girl? Yuck."

"Yeah, well, you'll see things differently in a few years." Miranda couldn't help smiling. "Just look at him. Those eyes . . . those lips . . ."

"Yuck!" Lynn repeated firmly. "He *never* laughs. He *never* talks. All he does is squint his eyes and try to look tough."

"He *is* tough."

"He probably can't even fight in real life. I bet someone else does his fight scenes for him."

"For your information, he does most of his own stunts himself," Miranda said indignantly. "Not that he'd have to do *anything* else to look totally gorgeous—"

"I bet someone else does his kissing scenes, too. I bet he can't even kiss. I bet he's afraid of girls."

"Does this look like a guy who's intimidated by women? Wait—wait—here's the kiss."

Lynn made a gagging sound in her throat. "You and your friends are so stupid. I bet you think he's some kind of *hero* in real life. I bet you even think you're gonna win that stupid contest you entered."

Miranda shot her an angry glance. "You promised not to say anything about that to anyone."

"See? Even *you* think it's stupid, entering that contest."

"Someone has to win it," Miranda reminded her irritably. "It might as well be me."

"Your chances are about one in a zillion," Lynn scoffed. "And anyway, what would you do if you *did* win? He's probably a loser. Probably some big stupid stuck-up macho loser. You'd probably hate him."

"I'd like a chance to find out for myself, if you don't mind."

"You don't *honestly* think you *have* that chance, do you? Can you imagine how many girls entered that magazine contest? Every girl in the whole country! Maybe every girl in the whole world!"

Miranda bestowed her a chilly smile. "Maybe you're exaggerating. Just a little."

"'Win a week with Byron Slater,'" Lynn mimicked. "'Just send in the entry blank, and *you* might be the lucky girl who gets to co-star in his new movie!' Yeah, right. Like *that* would really happen to anyone."

"No one's interested in your opinion."

Exasperated, Miranda began to rewind the video. Deep down she hated to admit it, but Lynn *was* right about one thing—she was embarrassed now to think she'd ever gotten so excited over that advertisement in *On the Edge* magazine. God, how she wished she could win that contest! She'd read that article on Byron Slater at least twenty times before she'd finally filled out the entry form—and then she'd secretly mailed it off the next morning. She hadn't told anyone—not her parents, not even her best friend, Amy—she'd been so embarrassed about it. She wouldn't have told Lynn, either, only Lynn had been going through her purse and found the entry hidden there.

"I bet *On the Edge* won't pick anyone's name," Lynn went on now. "I bet it was just a stupid trick to get more dumb girls to buy their magazine."

Miranda started to snap back at her, paused, then gave a grudging nod.

"Oh, you're probably right," she grumbled. "There probably won't even *be* three semifinalists. Or if there are, it'll be *fixed*, so three beautiful, perfect girls who all *know* someone at the magazine will be flying off to California to stay at Byron Slater's estate."

"Beautiful and perfect? That lets you out."

Miranda wound a strand of hair around one slim finger. Her blue eyes narrowed in disgust. "The closest I'll ever get to winning is reading about everything in the next issue."

"Even if someone *does* get to go, it won't matter. I've read articles about Byron Slater, too, you know." Lynn nodded her head wisely. "They all say he's quiet and private and hates reporters. And he's always beating them up."

"You don't know if that's true or not. Maybe they were bothering him. Most reporters are really rude."

"And he's always involved with a million different women."

"You can't believe that, either. Tabloids will print anything. He's probably a really nice person."

"Oh, sure. Nobody can be that rich and famous and not be a total jerk." Lynn's expression went smug. "Miranda, sometimes you do really dumb things, but this is absolutely the *dumbest.*"

The video clicked to a halt. Miranda ejected it from the VCR and began to hunt for the box to put it away. Lynn changed the channel on the TV, punched up the volume, then turned at a sound from the kitchen.

"Phone!" she yelled, bounding from the couch. "I'll get it!"

Miranda ignored her. She held up the video and stared at the photo of Byron Slater on the front of the box. Tall, leanly muscled, coal black hair, dark black eyes, that hard, intense stare off into the distance, as he planned out his next move against the bad guys. All coolness and aloofness and total control. And totally sexy, Miranda thought—she'd never seen a guy who exuded such easy, effortless sexuality. No wonder he'd risen so fast in the ranks of box-office phenomena; no wonder millions of starry-eyed females fantasized about him.

Miranda sighed again and put the video back in

the cabinet. *Lynn's probably right,* she thought to herself. *What do I care about the contest anyway? He probably* is *a total jerk.*

She jumped as a shriek echoed through the kitchen.

"Lynn?" she called, starting through the living room. "Lynn, are you all right?"

And she saw her little sister rooted there in the doorway, clutching the phone in one hand, the freckles standing out on her flushed, excited face.

"Lynn, what's wrong—"

"It's that *magazine!*" Lynn sputtered, waving the receiver, her voice shaking out of control.

"What? What are you—"

"The *magazine! On the Edge* magazine!" Lynn fairly threw the phone at Miranda, then grabbed her in a suffocating hug. "Oh, Miranda!" she squealed. "The *contest!* The Byron Slater *contest! You won!"*

2

"I can't believe we're so late," Lucille grumbled. "I mean, here you are on the trip of a lifetime, and our plane gets grounded!"

"It wasn't your fault," Miranda replied good-naturedly. "And at least they put us on another flight. I'm just glad we finally got here at all."

"Got here in one piece, you mean!" Lucille exclaimed. With a firm grip on Miranda's elbow, the editor of *On the Edge* began weaving through the crowded airport. "Of all times to have bad weather and broken planes—"

"But see? The weather's perfect now." Miranda motioned toward the windows, to the California sun shining brightly in at them. Lucille barely gave it a glance.

"The party's already started." She sighed. "You're

one of the important guests, and they're having fun without you."

"It's really okay," Miranda soothed again. "And thanks for escorting me, Lucille. My folks were so weird about that, you'd think I was *seven,* not seventeen. I was afraid I wouldn't get to come. I don't mind being late." Mind? How could she possibly mind! She was *here,* wasn't she?—in California, with an editor from *On the Edge* magazine, on her way to Byron Slater's estate! How could she mind about anything?

"Where's the stupid driver?" Lucille fretted, peering off into the crowds. "Do you see anyone standing around? Holding a sign with your name on it? An old guy with a crew cut who's not wearing his chauffeur's cap?"

Miranda scanned the area, but shook her head. "Maybe he left when our flight didn't show up."

"He couldn't have left, I called on our layover. Now, I don't want you to worry—"

"I'm not worrying," Miranda promised, but Lucille rushed on.

"I mean, this is *your* week! You're not supposed to worry about anything."

"I'm not worrying," Miranda insisted, more firmly this time. "As a matter of fact, I'm too numb to worry. I think I'm in shock. I still can't believe this is all happening."

"Well, believe it." Lucille threw her a look, then patted Miranda's shoulder. "You're a trouper, you know that? Some girls would be whining and complaining and making my job miserable. Believe me, I speak from experience. Every time we run a big contest like this, I *always* get stuck with the prima donnas!"

Before Miranda could answer, Lucille began dragging her toward a luggage carousel. A huge mob had already gathered around it, but Lucille plunged right through, hauling Miranda with her.

"I just want you to know I won't be hanging around playing chaperon the whole time, okay?" Lucille went on, scanning the conveyor belt with a practiced eye. "My job was to talk to your folks, convince them that *On the Edge* is on the up and up, and come with you on the plane. But now that we're here, I'm sure you won't care if I keep a low profile!" She pointed toward a cluster of luggage. "Is one of those yours?"

"No. I don't see it yet."

"Maybe we should get closer, huh?"

As Lucille pushed ahead, Miranda felt something touch her shoulder.

"Miss Peterson?"

She whirled around. Standing behind her was a tall young man, somewhere in his early to mid-twenties, she supposed, who was dressed in the strangest combination she'd ever seen. Baggy black pants had been cut off just below his knees, and he wore a rumpled white dress shirt, red socks, orange tennis shoes, and a chauffeur's cap.

"Miss Peterson?" he asked again. "Miranda Peterson?"

Before Miranda could answer, Lucille was there again, stepping boldly between them.

"You Byron Slater's driver?" she demanded.

The young man flashed an amused grin. "The one and only."

"Since when? I've *seen* his driver, and you're not him."

"Since a month ago when he drove to that big garage in the sky."

"What!" Lucille gasped. "Pete *died?*"

"Well, you know." The young man shrugged. "He was old. But it's okay—I'm a good friend of Byron's."

"That consoles me. Where's Miguel?"

"Who?"

"Miguel? The photographer? There's supposed to be a photographer here with you."

"There's no one here but me."

"Well, isn't that just great—they've screwed up already." Lucille rolled her eyes, then shrugged. "Well, what took you so long, driver? We've been here for *hours!*"

"Liar." He grinned again, and Lucille burst out laughing.

"Well, come on, then," she told him, motioning in Miranda's direction. "Miss Peterson's tired and hungry and dying of anticipation."

"I don't have my suitcase yet," Miranda reminded her, and Lucille immediately slapped a palm to her forehead.

"Where's my head? Better yet, where's your suitcase?"

"Don't worry about the suitcase," the young man said quickly. "Why don't you ladies go wait in the car, and I'll bring it out. What's it look like?"

"No, I've got a better idea," Lucille decided, taking hold of Miranda's arm, pulling her over to the wall. "Where's your camera, Miranda? I'll take a picture of you with—with—" She stopped and squinted at the driver. "Who are you?"

"Nick."

"Of course you are. Nick who?"

"Howard."

Lucille frowned, as though trying to remember something. "Hmmm . . . that name sounds so familiar. Howard . . . Howard . . . I know!" She snapped her fingers. "You're the Nick that Byron talked about in one of our interviews."

"I want to know what he said about me before I confirm that," Nick returned offhandedly.

"I never forget a name." Lucille looked proud of herself. "He *did* say you were friends, that you two go back a few years. Okay, Nick. You and Miranda stand right over there."

"Lucille," Miranda protested, her cheeks flushing. "What are you doing?"

"Don't you want photos of your trip?" Lucille looked surprised. "Look—we get the airport, the driver, the whole beginning. You *do* want to remember all the details, don't you?"

"Well . . . yes . . . but . . ."

"Oh, come on, I won't bite." Nick flashed that cute grin and draped one arm around Miranda's shoulders, pulling her back against his chest. "Just smile and say 'vacation.'"

"I really need to watch for my suitcase," Miranda protested again, but Lucille waved her off and held up the camera.

"Okay, okay, that's a good one! I've got it! Now wait—I'll take some with my camera, too. Just in case."

"Really, I think this is fine," Miranda assured her, but Nick's hold around her tightened.

"Humor her," he mumbled in Miranda's ear. "Otherwise we might be here all night."

Miranda saw the flash go off, and Nick started to laugh.

"Good one!" he cheered. "Too bad we weren't in it!"

"That's enough from you!" Lucille warned. She planted her feet firmly apart and aimed the lens straight at them. Nick waved one arm, and this time Lucille managed to snap the picture.

"Wonderful!" Lucille beamed, immensely proud of herself. "Miranda, is that enough—or do you want some more?"

"That's plenty." Miranda flushed again, all too conscious of Nick's hand sliding down her arm, the warm path it traced on her bare skin.

"My pleasure, ladies." Nick touched a finger to the brim of his cap. "Anything to make your trip more enjoyable."

Without another word, he picked up their things and began sauntering toward the exit. His hair looked soft and silky, sun-bleached nearly white. It swung loosely over his shoulder blades, a sharp contrast to the deep bronze of his tan.

"Hmmm . . . nice view," Lucille whispered, and Miranda choked back a laugh.

"Actually, I was thinking the same thing," she admitted.

If Nick heard the comment, he gave no sign. He helped them into the limousine, took the description of Miranda's suitcase, and then, with that same slightly amused expression, went back inside the airport.

Ten minutes passed. Lucille lounged back in the cushy seat, chatting about other magazine assignments she'd had, speculating about what this one held in store. But when ten more minutes dragged by and Nick hadn't returned, Miranda grew anxious.

"Maybe I should go in there. Maybe he can't find it," she worried, but Lucille opened the door and got out.

"I had a feeling this guy was totally worthless." Lucille chuckled. "Maybe he's out of work and Byron felt sorry for him."

"What do you mean?"

"The two of them started out together in acting school and got to be great friends. Later on they were both up for a big part—one that Nick especially had his heart set on—only Byron ended up getting it instead. I guess Nick took it pretty hard."

"That's so sad. But couldn't Nick get other parts?"

Lucille gave her a sympathetic look. "I think he was told at the time that he really didn't have what it takes to make it in this business."

"Who told him that? And why did he believe it?"

"Oh, Miranda, this is a cruel place. People love to break your heart . . . and your dreams. Less competition that way. And I'm guessing it sure couldn't have helped much, Byron getting bigger and bigger and leaving Nick behind."

"And Byron told you all this?"

Lucille nodded. "I think he probably feels a little guilty. The good news is, they're still friends, so I guess that's the important thing." She laughed and motioned toward the airport. "So on to the missing suitcase! I'll be right back!"

Again Miranda waited. After fifteen more minutes she saw Nick come outside, but without any suitcase. He bounded off the curb, landed in front of an oncoming car, then held up his hand in a casual wave as the driver leaned angrily on his horn.

"You could have been killed!" Miranda greeted him as he leaned inside the back door.

Nick only grinned. "Won't happen. I'm invincible."

"Where's Lucille? Where's my suitcase?"

"There's Lucille," he announced as the woman came hurrying from another exit. "But I'm afraid your suitcase didn't make it."

"Oh, no!" Miranda groaned. "Please don't tell me that."

Nick thought a minute, then shrugged. "Okay. Pretend I never said it."

"You *are* kidding, aren't you?" Lucille spoke up. "After all the other travel horrors we've been through today?"

Nick looked genuinely sorry. "No bags left to be claimed. I even checked in the office."

"What am I going to do?" Miranda slid lower in the seat, and Lucille reached over, patting her consolingly.

"Now, relax," Lucille soothed. "We'll find you some clothes. No big deal—"

14

"No big deal? I don't have anything to wear, and you say it's no big deal?"

"You don't need clothes," Nick deadpanned. "You're in California, remember?"

"I'll have to give them a description of my bag," Miranda said, but Nick stopped her before she could get out.

"I already took care of it. Description and claim number. They said they'd run it by the house later on. When they find it."

"Don't you mean *if* they find it?" Miranda sighed.

"Come on now, it's not a disaster," Lucille assured her. "Airlines lose luggage all the time. And besides, you're going to get a makeover, and that includes a whole new wardrobe!"

Miranda hesitated . . . glanced at Lucille's reassuring smile . . . nodded reluctantly. "You're right. They'll probably have it to me in a few hours."

"Then let's move," Nick said cheerfully. He slid into the front and started the engine. "Help yourself, ladies—the backseat's fully stocked."

"Perrier?" Lucille suggested, opening up the little refrigerator. "Chocolates? Some smoked almonds, perhaps?"

"Diet Coke?" Miranda asked tentatively. She couldn't see Nick's face, but she had the distinct feeling he was laughing.

The ride seemed endless, but incredibly beautiful. Miranda wished Lucille would stop talking just long enough for her to actually concentrate on the passing scenery. Through the limousine's tinted windows she caught glimpses of steep, narrow highway and patches of cloudless sky, and from time to time a sheer drop to the jagged coastline far below, where water pounded and surged over the rocks. As they wound higher and higher up into the mountains, there were also brilliant bursts of flowering color through the trees, and then lengthening beams of late sunlight easing slowly down toward the horizon. After what seemed like hours she felt the car slow down again and turn off onto an even narrower road, which continued upward for a distance of several more miles.

Then "Here we are," Nick announced. "Welcome to Slaterland."

"Slaterland? Is that really what it's called?" Miranda whispered, but before Lucille could answer, tall iron gates hummed back on either side of the road, and they were slipping through.

The gates slid back behind them.

Nick winked at her in the rearview mirror.

"Got you, Miranda," he said softly. "There's no way you can get out of here now."

3

He was kidding, of course.

Only kidding, Miranda told herself. Teasing her like he'd teased her back there at the airport.

And yet . . .

Miranda felt a strange little chill snake upward along her spine.

"Like she'd ever *want* to get out." Lucille chuckled, nudging Miranda back to the present. "Like any girl in her right mind would *ever* want to get away when she could be locked in here with Byron Slater."

Nick smiled and averted his eyes.

The limousine rolled smoothly to a stop.

"There's the house," Nick said. "Just look straight through those trees."

Miranda looked and, at the same time, thought surely she must be dreaming.

Things like this existed only in books and

movies—in the wildest dreams, in the most wonderful realms of imagination—but never, *never* in real life—and certainly not in *hers*. . . .

She could see the whiteness of it, the grandness of it, going on and on forever, like some majestic palace, rooftops and gables and columns and balconies, skylights and sundecks and hundreds of windows, it seemed like. Lush green trees and flowers blooming everywhere she looked. Spanish tiles and trellises and tall silvery sprays of water—fountains and pools and miniature waterfalls and—

"Close your mouth, Miranda." Nick glanced back over his shoulder. "It's not *cool* around here to be impressed."

Miranda flushed and settled back in the seat. She could hear Lucille laughing, and she kept her eyes on the window as Nick urged the car along the winding drive. For just a second she thought she'd detected a note of sarcasm in Nick's voice. Sarcasm just beneath the surface of his joke.

They stopped at last. The house loomed above them in full view, and as Nick opened their doors and began collecting their things, the two women got out.

"I know what you're thinking," Lucille mumbled. "But believe me, this is small potatoes, compared to some of the stars I've interviewed."

"You're joking."

"I never joke about money. Come on."

Lucille linked her arm through Miranda's, and together they followed Nick up the wide steps of a veranda. Before they'd even reached the door, it was opened by an elegant young woman with platinum hair and steel-gray eyes who gave Nick a decidedly chilly smile.

"I suppose you got lost?" she addressed him.

"If I'd known *you* were going to be here, I sure would've," he countered smoothly. "Ladies, this is Peg Carter, Byron's publicist. Peg, meet Lucille and—"

"On the Edge magazine, of course. Lucille and I have spoken frequently by phone." So saying, Peg breezed straight over to Miranda and offered her a slim, perfectly manicured hand. "Miranda. Our guest of honor."

"Well, one of them," Miranda corrected politely, but Peg drew her away from Lucille and began leading her into the house.

"You're very late," she scolded mildly. "Everyone's already at the reception."

Miranda opened her mouth to explain, but Peg didn't give her a chance.

"Byron's on a tight schedule," the publicist went on firmly. "He's doing a movie now, so naturally, any time he's able to spend with his guests will be quite limited. That's why it's so important to be prompt. Now let me go over some basic rules, so that when you *do* meet Byron Slater—"

"God, Peg," Nick groaned. "Give it a rest, will you?"

Before Peg could reply, a dark, hulking shadow suddenly fell across them from the entryway. Surprised, Miranda looked up to see a swarthy young man staring back at her. He was enormous—not fat, by any means—but thick and brawny and muscular, with a height easily close to seven feet, and a square, unsmiling face with thick black brows and a long, droopy black mustache. Without a word he stepped up to Miranda and began going over her with a handheld metal detector.

"Hey!" Miranda exclaimed, jumping back angrily. "What do you think you're doing!"

"It's strictly routine," Peg assured her, a little impatiently. "Naturally, no one can come in without being searched."

"Routine?" Miranda stared at her.

"Of course. All stars of Byron's caliber have personal bodyguards and security. One can't be too careful, you know."

"And if you don't like Harley's technique"—Nick glanced innocently at Miranda—"I'd be glad to volunteer for a more hands-on approach."

Miranda looked back at Lucille, who was trying desperately to hide a smile.

"Harley?" Miranda murmured, stifling a laugh of her own.

"Harley, this is Miranda Peterson," Peg said crisply. "Our third and final guest."

"Nice to meet you, Harley." Somehow Miranda managed to keep her voice normal. Harley fixed her with an unblinking stare, planted his feet apart, and folded his beefy arms across his chest.

"Oh. Harley doesn't talk," Nick explained in a loud stage whisper. "So don't take it personally." He dropped the luggage he was carrying and stretched his arms above his head. "Hurry, Harley. Me next. I've been waiting for this all day."

Harley's eyes narrowed in a silent glare. Nick

grinned, picked up the bags again, and sauntered past him into the foyer.

"I'm sure you'll want a little time," Peg said, pausing at the foot of a winding staircase. Her gaze went quickly over Miranda, while she added, "Freshen your makeup . . . change your clothes, no doubt."

"Well, actually—" Miranda began, but the woman rushed on.

"And I hope you're not camera-shy. We've planned lots of publicity this week, and one of the girls practically runs and hides every time a photographer gets near her."

"Miranda's very photogenic," Lucille spoke up. "She's a natural for the camera."

"Is that so, Miranda?" Nick feigned shock. "You're going to pose au naturel for the camera?"

This time Miranda did laugh. She glanced from Nick back to Peg and shrugged her shoulders. "Look, the airline lost my suitcase. I don't have any other clothes, and my mascara's in transit somewhere. So this is the only face I've got, whether I freshen it or not."

There was a long moment of silence.

"Well," Peg said.

"Deep subject for a shallow mind," Nick stated.

Peg's imperious gaze swept over him as though he were nothing more than a speck on the wall.

"Well," Peg said again. "I certainly didn't mean to imply—"

"What's the problem, Peg?"

It was a new voice that spoke now—a different

voice, deep and soft and slightly husky, that came from the sunken living room off to their side. And yet Miranda would have recognized it anywhere. As Byron Slater walked up the steps and into the hall, she put a hand casually to her throat, certain that everyone would notice the wild racing of her pulse.

He was even handsomer in real life.

Much handsomer and much taller, too, than in his films.

Miranda watched as he moved toward them. To her surprise, there was none of that cockiness, none of that attitude that always sparked from him on the big screen. Instead he looked solemn, even gentle, she thought, and in spite of the thick stubble on his angular cheeks, there was something almost boyish about him.

He stopped several feet away, assessing them with one smooth glance, and in that instant Miranda could have sworn she saw something flicker in his dark, dark eyes. Curiosity? Confusion? Whatever it might have been, in the very next second it was gone, replaced by polite detachment.

"Here's Lucille," Peg announced loudly, as though Byron must be totally deaf as well as blind. "You remember Lucille? From *On the Edge* magazine?"

"Lucille. Of course. How are you?" Byron reached out with a handshake, his eyes warming and melting as he smiled that famous smile. Miranda's heart stuck fast in her throat.

"I'm exhausted!" Lucille exclaimed delightedly. "And what about you? You look pretty done in yourself."

He stepped back, nodding, folding his arms over his chest. His eyes flashed briefly to Miranda's face, down her body, then away again, and she took that moment to steal another look at him. Tight faded jeans. White T-shirt. The solid width of his shoulders, the sinewy muscles of his arms . . .

"I am tired," Byron admitted. "I just got home about two minutes ago."

"No kidding?" Lucille sounded surprised. "Where've you been?"

"Italy," Byron replied.

"Boy, you *do* keep a tight schedule, don't you?" Lucille laughed. "From one pressing engagement to another!"

"So what exactly is—" Byron began, but Peg stepped between them, turning Byron around so that he faced Miranda.

"And this is Miranda Peterson," Peg said cheerfully. "She's one of the girls who'll be staying with us!"

Again Byron looked at her, only this time his gaze remained upon her face. "Miranda. Hello," he said. Then, glancing at Peg, "Staying with us? Peg, would you like to tell me what's going—"

"Miranda Peterson," Lucille echoed. "One of the three contest winners! And what a week we've planned for all of you—right, Byron?"

"Miranda Peterson," Peg added firmly, nodding in Miranda's direction.

Miranda saw Byron reach out . . . saw his strong, slender fingers close around her own. To her surprise, she felt an unexpected current pass between them, hot and cold sensations coursing through her

23

body. For a long moment she stood there, staring down at his arm, but when Nick gave a loud cough, she roused herself and met Byron's eyes.

"Yes. Yes, hi," she heard herself say. "I'm . . . Miranda."

"So I've been told." Byron raised an eyebrow and stared at Peg.

Nick coughed again. Miranda could have sworn he muttered, "Not cool," under his breath.

"Well . . . I'm . . . so glad you're here, Miranda." Byron gave her fingers a quick squeeze, then lifted one hand in a casual wave. "Let us know if you need anything."

Miranda nodded. She glanced at Nick and saw him roll his eyes.

"Thanks, I will," she answered. But at least her voice sounded stronger now—almost normal and halfway sane. *Get a grip, Miranda!* "Long life," she added offhandedly.

It came out before she thought—before she realized she was even thinking it. She stopped, biting her lip, as everyone turned to stare at her.

"Excuse me?" Byron asked.

"I said, long life," Miranda repeated, again before she could help herself. "The line on your palm. The lifeline."

Oh, my God, what have I done?

Peg and Nick and Byron and Lucille—even Harley, who'd suddenly appeared again and was standing close to Byron's elbow—all of them just staring at her, just staring at her as if she was crazy—

That's it, Miranda, you've ruined it. You might as well just turn around and walk right out of here.

*Before they call someone with a straitjacket to haul
you away.*

"Byron, you really should be getting to the party,"
Peg reminded him.

"Party?" Byron stared at her. *"What* party, Peg? I
just *got* here, remember?"

Peg shot an anxious look at Nick, and then at
Harley, but Byron didn't seem to notice.

"You read palms?" He was staring at Miranda,
and his face was softly quizzical.

Miranda forced a laugh. "Doesn't everyone?"

Byron shook his head.

"No? Not any of you?" Miranda glanced at each
person in turn. All of them shook their heads.
"Well"—she shrugged—"it's just a little hobby of
mine."

She wondered if her cheeks were red, if she was
giving herself away. *Miranda, you liar!* She and Amy
had found a book about three months ago, had
studied this book about palm reading, and then
practiced on each other. That was the extent of her
palm-reading ability!

But Byron was still looking at her, his eyes dark
and curious upon her face, even as someone called to
him from the other room, even as he started backing
away.

"I'd like to talk about that," he said.

Miranda managed a casual nod. "Well . . . sure."

"I really mean it," Byron insisted.

"Byron, don't you think—" Peg started, but Byron held up one hand, cutting her off.

"Where's Miranda staying?" he asked with a
frown.

25

"Well, out in the guesthouse, naturally, with the others—"

"Maybe she'd be more comfortable here in one of the spare rooms."

"But, Byron—" Again that anxious expression on Peg's face, that glance passed to Nick, to Harley, which Byron seemed so oblivious to. "But, Byron," Peg tried again, "the other girls have rooms in the guesthouse, and somehow I think it might be better if—"

"Upstairs," Byron said quietly. "Put her upstairs, Peg."

An uncomfortable silence fell. Byron peered earnestly into Miranda's face.

"I'd like to hear more about my lifeline," he said again.

And Miranda, suddenly all too conscious of Peg's hateful glare, heard herself answer, "Sure. Whenever you want."

4

"Want some advice?" Nick asked.

Slinging Miranda's totebag over his back, he took the plush stairs two at a time. Miranda tried gamely to keep up with him.

"Would it matter if I said no?" she panted.

"Believe me, I have only your best interest at heart. You *don't* want to be accessible. Not to Byron. And certainly not to Peg."

"Why would you even say that?"

"Look, you seem like a nice girl. I'm only thinking of your reputation. And your life."

"What are you talking about?"

"Let's just say Peg's a little . . . territorial. She and Byron had—at one time—a very, very, very, very, *very* close—uh—business association."

Miranda reached the top of the stairway at last. She frowned at Nick, her voice bristling. "I don't

27

know what you're suggesting, but I can take care of myself, thanks very much!"

"And I believe you," Nick countered, that amused grin spreading over his face. "Follow me."

He led her down a long carpeted hallway, talking softly as they went.

"Let me brief you so you don't make a fool of yourself at the party—"

"Excuse me?"

"Well, you've managed to do a pretty good job already."

Miranda stopped. She put her hands on her hips and glared at him as he swung back to face her. "And just what's that supposed to mean?"

"What?" Nick asked innocently.

"That little remark you just made!"

"Oh, come on, you're no palm reader. I've heard more lines than you'll ever hear in ten lifetimes. Girls will say anything—*do* anything—just to get close to Byron Slater."

"So you think I'm lying?"

Nick chuckled. "Give me a break, Miranda."

"Well, Byron believed me."

"No, he didn't. You're just the kind of girl he always falls for."

Miranda felt her heart plunge to the pit of her stomach.

"*Always* falls for?"

"Sure. What'd you think? That you'd be any different from any of the other girls that end up staying here? *Upstairs? In* the house?"

She stared at him. For a split second she heard

Lynn's voice echoing through her brain—*"and he's always involved with a million different women."*

"You're just jealous," she said lamely.

Now it was Nick who stared. He held her eyes for an endless moment, then finally shrugged and gave a huge smile.

"You're right," he conceded. "I'm jealous."

He stopped and opened a door, looked in, then backed out again, motioning her on.

"Looks like this one's taken," Nick said. "I never know who's sleeping where in this crazy house. But if the other rooms up here aren't empty, you just might have to bunk with me."

"I'd rather sleep in the car," Miranda returned, but Nick didn't seem to hear.

"Okay." He glanced back over his shoulder. "Listen up, 'cause I'm only going through this once. Zena Hart is Byron's stylist—she's the one who'll be doing your fashion and shopping thing. Maria and Paul take care of the place—she's the housekeeper, and he oversees all the outside work. If you want anything, ask them. Or ask one of the maids running around—I can never remember all their names, but I think they're all sisters or cousins or something. You've already met Peg the Dread—and then there's Robert and—"

"You really expect me to remember all this?" Miranda broke in. "I'm only going to be here a week."

Nick looked slightly disgusted. "Right. Like you'd have trouble remembering the dialogue from every single one of Byron's movies."

"That's different."

"Yeah, that's what they all say."

Miranda tried to keep her voice casual. "How many of Byron's girlfriends *have* you known, anyway?"

"You're changing the subject. You'll like Robert—he's the only sane one around this place. Except me, of course."

"That's certainly comforting. Who's Robert?"

"Byron's agent. Well, here we are." Nick paused, pushed open a door, and motioned her in. "Your boudoir, Miss Peterson."

Miranda gasped at the sheer luxury of it. White wicker furniture filled the room, and the four-poster bed was hung with yards and yards of sheer mosquito netting. There were vases of fresh-cut flowers, and classical music floated softly from invisible speakers. Tall French doors opened out onto a balcony, their gauzy curtains fluttering in on a balmy breeze.

"It's so beautiful," Miranda breathed. "I've never seen anything like this."

"Close your mouth," Nick reminded her, tapping her gently on the chin. "Yeah, I have to admit, this place is really something, isn't it? It's really old and crumbly, too, in parts—so it's pretty amazing what they've done to it." He set her bag on the floor by the closet and walked across to the French doors, throwing them wide. "There's a hot tub out here for your private enjoyment. And you notice I stress the word *private.*"

"Would you stop?" Miranda bristled again.

"And there's a bell—here." Nick indicated it near the bed. "Ring if you want anything, or just pick up the phone. Kitchen's open twenty-four hours, and they *expect* you to order room service. But I'm sure someone will be in here to fill you in on the details."

"Where will you be?"

He looked surprised for a second. Then he put his hand on her back and guided her over to the balcony, pointing to a rooftop off behind some trees.

"See that? That's the garage. Well, one of them. I live right above there. As you can see, I'm pretty damn important."

Miranda smiled.

"So if you need me," Nick went on, "just come out on the balcony and yell. Or wave a red flag. Or send up smoke signals. Something."

"Thanks."

"Yeah, well, don't mention it."

They went back inside, and Nick continued with the orientation.

"Bathroom through there. Closet through there. Big-screen TV. Just in case you didn't notice."

"How could I not notice? It takes up the whole wall."

"There's a video library downstairs. In case there's something you want to watch in bed." He narrowed his eyes at her. *"Is* there someone—I mean, *something*—you'd like to watch in bed?"

Miranda tried unsucessfully to hide a smile. "Nothing comes to mind at the moment."

"Oh. Well, then, I guess I'll go."

Miranda watched him walk to the door. He put one hand on the doorknob, then he hesitated, staring down at the floor as if trying to reach some sort of decision.

"About Byron," he said softly.

To Miranda's surprise, Nick turned back to face her, his expression gone serious.

"What about Byron?" she asked.

Nick still seemed deep in thought. He took a step toward her, then stopped.

"He's a great guy," Nick said quietly. "A great friend, too. But he's got a lot on his mind right now . . . a lot of serious stuff going on in his life. So if he seems—"

Nick broke off. He stared at her uncertainly, then without another word, he let himself out into the hall, closing the door behind him.

Miranda stood there, puzzled. This wasn't the irreverent teasing, the blunt sarcasm she'd witnessed in Nick all afternoon—this was something entirely different. Something important. Upsetting, even.

But what?

She walked to the door and started to lock it, when suddenly there were footsteps out in the hallway.

"Nick!" a voice hissed. "What the hell's going on around here!"

There was no response. Miranda pressed her ear to the door and listened. For a minute she thought whoever it was had gone away.

And then she heard Nick's voice. Not so far from the door. Lowered, though, and very cautious.

"Why aren't you at the party? You're supposed to be meeting those girls—"

"What girls?" the voice answered, and Miranda strained to hear. Deep . . . and soft . . . and slightly husky . . . *Byron? Byron's voice?*

"Some magazine contest," Nick said lamely.

"Three girls won a week here with you, and one of them's supposed to get a part in your new movie."

"This is insane—why didn't somebody tell me? I come home to find a bunch of strangers running all over my house, and I'm supposed to entertain them? With all the bad stuff that's been going on around here?"

"Come on, Byron, there's nothing bad going on— you've just been working too hard, that's all. But you've had a vacation now, and things'll be better. You'll be fine."

"Don't humor me, Nick—one Peg around here is enough. I'm getting threats from some crazy fan, and you invite three *more* crazy fans right into my life—"

"Hey, it wasn't my idea! I didn't have anything to do with it!"

"Do you even know these girls? Does *anyone* know these girls? For all you know, they could be—"

"Wait," Nick murmured, cutting him off. "Not here, Byron. Someplace else we can talk."

But Byron didn't wait. He whispered again, very close to Miranda's door, his voice low and choked, so she could barely hear.

"How many times do I have to tell you— *someone's* after me. And she might not stop till I'm dead."

5

Miranda froze, one hand on the doorknob.

Dead? Is that what Byron had whispered so cautiously out in the hall? Or had she simply misunderstood, gotten the whole conversation wrong?

Very carefully Miranda turned the handle. She inched the door open and tried to peer out through the crack.

The hallway was empty. As she strained to hear, she thought there might have been a muffled fading of feet on carpet . . . the soft slamming of a door.

"Miranda?"

Miranda nearly jumped out of her skin. As a familiar face peered around the door, she stepped back and gave a relieved sigh.

"Lucille, you scared me to death!"

"Sorry," her friend greeted her. "I can't help it,

though. These carpets are great for sneaking around!"

"Did you see someone in the hall just now?"

Lucille glanced back over her shoulder, then shrugged. "No. Should I have?"

"Did you hear anyone talking?"

"Sorry. Is there some secret liaison going on that I should know about? Now remember—I promised your parents I'd look after you."

"What is this anyway?" Miranda demanded, taking another quick look down the empty corridor. "Why is everyone so concerned about my virtue all of a sudden?"

"Ah-hah! So there *is* something going on I should know about."

"There's nothing going on. I just thought I heard something, that's all."

As the two of them walked into the bedroom, Lucille surveyed their surroundings with a low whistle.

"Would you look at this? I'd say you rated *very* high, my dear."

"It *is* nice, isn't it." Miranda sighed. "But I don't feel right about being here. Wouldn't it be better if I stayed in the guesthouse, like Peg said?"

"Hold it, hold it!" Lucille put a hand over Miranda's mouth and shook her head in amusement. "Why are you even worried about this? *I* don't have a problem with it, okay? So you shouldn't, either. You've got a good head on your shoulders. Not the kind of head easily turned by an actor, I should think."

"Well, *Nick* seems to think—"

"Oh, Nick!" Lucille burst out with a laugh. "From what I've seen of Nick so far, I seriously doubt he thinks at all. Goodness! This is almost sinful!"

Lucille flopped on the edge of the king-size bed, bouncing up and down on the mattress as Miranda crossed to the French doors and gazed out across the balcony. She couldn't get Byron's voice—or the strange conversation—out of her mind. He'd sounded so urgent . . . so upset. He'd sounded frightened.

She leaned her head against the doorframe. She could see the rooftop Nick had pointed out; she could see one side of the garage showing beyond the trees. The windows were dark and empty. It'd be easy for someone to stand behind them and watch this balcony without her ever knowing.

Now, where did that come from? Miranda scolded herself. *What a stupid thing to even think about.*

"I just met your two competitors downstairs," Lucille said casually.

Miranda threw her an anxious glance. "They're probably as nervous as I am, right?"

"Hmmm." Lucille's eyes sparkled mischievously. "It wouldn't be fair—or professional—of me to offer any sort of opinion."

"Which means?"

"Which means . . ." Lucille rolled her head to the side and let out a luxurious sigh. "Which means I could get fired for saying this, but I really hope you win."

"You hope *I* do?"

"Absolutely. They're not Byron's type at all."

"Lucille!"

"I know, I know, I'm way out of line. And the decision's not up to me anyhow."

"I thought the magazine decided."

"Nope. Guess again."

"Byron's people? That Peg person?"

"No. Just Byron. Still, I wanted you to know how *I* feel about it."

Miranda wrapped her arms about her chest, leveling a gaze at Lucille. "I bet you've said the same thing to those other two girls. I bet that's part of your job."

"Let me tell you something," Lucille answered. She pulled herself into a sitting position and gave a leisurely stretch. "There are *many* unpleasant things I'm forced to do as part of my job, but getting to know you certainly hasn't been one of them."

Miranda laughed. "You *don't* know me."

"Of course I know you. We've just spent the whole day traveling together, and before that, I spent hours with you on the phone. I'm an *expert* at knowing people, and knowing them fast. I was the first one to ever interview Byron, did I tell you that?"

"No kidding?"

Lucille smiled fondly, remembering. "He was a nobody then, with big hopeful dreams. I came away from that assignment feeling almost sorry for him."

"Why?"

"Because he was so sweet. He was kind and polite and really seemed to care about people. I never thought he'd last very long. I figured this business would eat him alive before he even had a chance to make it."

"But it didn't." Miranda sounded almost smug.

"Didn't it?"

"Well . . . no. I mean, *look* at him!"

"Yes. *Do* look at him." Lucille shook her head slowly. "Tell me what you see in his eyes, Miranda. He's come so far, so fast. And sometimes his eyes seem so . . . I don't know, exactly. Lonely, I guess. Or maybe *longing* is a better word."

In spite of the warm breeze, Miranda shivered. Again she heard Byron's voice from the hallway, echoing softly through her mind . . . *"She might not stop till I'm dead."*

"Miranda?" Lucille was watching her intently, and Miranda forced a smile.

"Sorry. Guess I'm just tired."

"You can't be tired. Tiredness isn't allowed this whole week." Lucille thought a moment, then added, "I like Byron—a *lot*. But sometimes I can't help but worry about him. And I know Robert does, too."

"Robert," Miranda mused. "His agent?"

"You've met him?"

"No, Nick was just filling me in on who's who."

"You'll love Robert, everyone does. Such a regular guy. And do you know he and I both hail from Chicago? He used to sell cars, for God's sake—and now he's rich!"

Miranda gave a faint smile. "Because of Byron."

"Well . . . I imagine there are quite a *lot* of people whose livelihoods depend on Byron." There was no mistaking the sarcasm in Lucille's tone, but then she added, "At least Robert's not one of the materialistic ones; he gives most of his money to charity. He even got Byron to leave big bucks for medical research in his will."

"Byron's will?" Miranda clarified, and Lucille nodded.

"Robert's amazing. He's a tireless crusader, and he's *very* generous if it's a cause he believes in."

Miranda mulled this over. "So what you're really saying is . . . everyone's using Byron."

"Is that what I'm saying?" Lucille frowned, then shrugged her shoulders. "Look, all celebrities get used; it comes with the territory. That's why it's so important to keep them grounded in the real world, so they don't forget who they are." Lucille paused, then pointed a finger at Miranda. "Byron's crazy if he doesn't pick you."

"Will you stop?" Miranda felt the heat rise in her cheeks. "You don't even know what Byron's interested in—or what he needs. Or what he's looking for," she added lamely.

"The question *is*"—Lucille sighed—"does *Byron?*" She stretched again, got to her feet, and held out both hands to Miranda. "Come on. You've got people to impress and pictures to pose for. There are lots of photographers, studio people, agents, some hangers-on, the works! Let's go!"

"Okay, okay, one minute." Miranda ducked in front of a mirror and ran her fingers recklessly through her hair. Then she swiped at her face with a tissue, frowned at her reflection, and turned back to Lucille. "Good thing I'm not hung up on looks."

"Good thing you don't live out *here!*" Lucille

laughed. "Prepare yourself, my dear. Tonight you're going to be subjected to more egos than you ever *dreamed* could exist in one place."

The reception was out by the pool. As Miranda followed Lucille onto the terrace, she felt her breath catch in her throat and tried not to gape at the exotic wonderland around her.

She'd never seen such total perfection. Perfectly placed tables with fluttering cloths of white linen, perfectly designed flower arrangements, trays of food all perfectly displayed like fine works of art and tended by servers wearing perfect white uniforms. The swimming pool shimmered a perfect blue, reflecting all around off handpainted tiles, while marble statues stood gracefully along every side, their perfectly sculpted bodies wound with tiny twinkling lights. There were lanterns strung at perfect intervals throughout the lush gardens, glowing softly in the gathering twilight. *And even the guests look perfect,* Miranda thought with dry amusement. Expensive clothes and hairstyles, not to mention those perfect smiles and tans.

Well, what did you expect? Taking a deep breath, she walked with Lucille through the laughing, chattering crowds, moving toward one group in particular.

"Girls," Lucille announced, linking her arm through Miranda's, "meet Miranda Peterson. Your friendly competition."

The two young women regarded her with polite smiles. Miranda returned them with one of her own.

"Miranda, this is Kelly McCormick and Jo

Brown. You three will be seeing a lot of each other this next week."

"Hi," Miranda said warmly, reaching out, shaking each girl's hand in turn.

"Hi, yourself," Jo acknowledged. She was short and round, with a firm, sincere handshake, and green eyes that twinkled back at Miranda from behind owlish glasses. "We were starting to wonder if you were going to get here at all."

"Plane trouble." Miranda grimaced, and Jo's smile widened.

"Always when you're in a hurry to get somewhere," Jo replied sympathetically. "Never when you're trying to kill time."

Laughing in agreement, Miranda glanced over at Kelly. The girl's expression hadn't changed, and she held herself stiff and aloof, as though posing for some invisible camera. She had model's cheekbones, flawless skin, and long, lustrous black hair, and Miranda suspected that if Kelly even *breathed* too hard, her pouty expression would shatter into a thousand little pieces.

Miranda glanced back at Jo and caught a sly, secretive wink.

"Well," Lucille said, taking a step back, "good luck to all of you. I'm sure no matter *who* wins a part in Byron's movie, we'll all enjoy making new friends!"

Jo looked as if she was trying not to laugh. Kelly lifted her chin and bestowed Lucille a regal, restrained smile.

Great, Miranda thought. *I'm stuck here for a whole week with some girl who hates my guts.*

She started to say something amiable to Kelly, but instead found herself looking at the girl's back. While Miranda watched in surprise, Kelly sashayed over to another group of people—one which included Peg, Miranda was quick to note. It took her a second to realize that someone was tugging on her arm.

"Want some shrimp?" Jo whispered. "I'm dying of hunger. I haven't eaten since this morning."

Miranda nodded, and they made their way over to one of the tables. Jo took a plate, heaped it with spiced shrimp, took one bite, and let out a blissful sigh.

"I was afraid I'd pass out if I had to wait another hour for food."

"When'd you get here?" Miranda asked, attacking her own plate with equal enthusiasm.

"This morning at ten—can you believe it? In fact, my flight got in just half an hour before the Princess did."

"The—oh." Miranda gave a knowing nod. "You mean Kelly."

"Or perhaps," Jo added, raising her nose haughtily in the air, "I should say *queen?*"

Miranda nodded again. "She doesn't seem very friendly."

"Friendly?" Jo's eyes widened in mock alarm. "She hasn't said a dozen words to me all day. But hey, who am *I*, anyway? When there're so many more *important* people around here to kiss up to?"

The two girls stared at each other, then burst out laughing. It felt good to laugh, Miranda realized, good to let out all the tension that had been building all day. Happily she gulped down five more shrimp, while Jo let out another contented sigh.

"My stomach is extremely pleased right now, Miranda. And frankly, if I'm going to be stuck here a whole week with the queen, I've got to find *some* humor in the situation, or I'll go crazy."

Miranda eased down into a chair, balancing her plate on her knees. "I know what you mean. I feel as if I'm in some weird dream or something. That someone's going to pinch me and wake me up."

"If only it were that easy." Jo rolled her eyes. "I'd give anything to wake up and be home again."

"Are you serious?" Miranda regarded her in surprise. "Aren't you excited about being here?"

"Let me answer that truthfully, Miranda. Number one, like I'd have any sort of chance with the queen." Jo snorted. "Number two, like I even care!" She laughed a booming laugh and popped another shrimp into her mouth. "You know the real reason why I'm here? 'Cause some of my friends—actually, I'm now considering making them my *ex*-friends— entered my name in that stupid contest! I don't even *like* Byron Slater!"

The absurdity of the situation seemed to overcome Jo at this point. She laughed heartily for several minutes, then wiped one hand across her eyes and took a deep breath.

"I can't swim, I never tan, I don't care one thing about clothes and makeup, and I'm terrible at conversation. The only good thing is that I've always wanted to see California. I figured this would be my one chance in life to get here."

The girls looked at each other, then burst into

fresh peals of laughter. As several people turned to stare at them, Jo affected her Kelly-like pose and lifted her nose high into the air.

"Be off with you," she said, waving her hand at the mystified onlookers. "Off with you, you peasants."

Miranda knew their behavior was out of line, but suddenly she didn't care. For all the perfect beauty and glamour of the place, it was also perfectly stuffy and stifling. Impulsively she grabbed Jo's arm, and said, "Let's make a deal."

"Name it." Jo grinned.

"Promise to keep each other sane while we're here."

"Deal."

They reached out and shook hands. Jo downed the last of her shrimp, then nodded off toward the party.

"Have you noticed that our host seems to be conspicuously absent?"

"As a matter of fact, I did notice that."

"How rude of him," Jo concluded. "Want to take a walk or something?"

"I thought you'd never ask."

A quick glance assured the girls that everyone else was much too busy to miss them. They wandered to the edge of the terrace and, after one last backward look, slipped off through a break in the shrubbery.

"This place is unreal." Jo shook her head in amazement as they wound deeper and deeper into the formal gardens. "Fountains . . . statues . . . sundials . . . look at all this stuff. Like some kind of paradise."

"Hmmm. I wonder."

44

"What do you mean by that?"

"Look." Miranda stopped and pointed. In the distance, rising high above fragrant foliage, they could see the top of a metal fence, oddly out of place with the peaceful elegance of their surroundings.

"Electrified," Jo murmured, and Miranda gave a nod. "Well, I guess if you're this famous, you can't be too careful."

"I guess."

The girls walked on in silence. Birds twittered softly, settling down for the night. Twilight crept over the gardens in a soft, muted haze, and lampposts began blinking on from strategic locations among the trees.

"I wonder who lived here before Byron Slater," Jo mused. "This just isn't the sort of place I expected an action hero to live in."

"Who knows? Maybe it belonged to some old movie-star idol of his. Or maybe he's not really the hard-core macho guy he pretends to be."

"Or maybe," Jo added thoughtfully, "he stays here because it's so isolated. I can't imagine anyone ever finding this place, can you?"

She went several steps ahead, then suddenly stopped and glanced back.

"Hey," she said quietly, "did you hear something?"

Miranda frowned. "No. What?"

"Just now . . . while I was walking." Jo frowned, too, and pointed toward a clump of bushes about six yards ahead of them. "It sounded like it came from there."

Miranda listened. The garden was silent now; even the birds were still, and shadows hovered thickly on every side.

"No," she replied cautiously, "I don't hear any—"

"Shhh!" Jo's voice rose in alarm. "There! Right *there!* Like something growling . . ."

"Yes. Yes, I hear it." Miranda moved up behind Jo and then stopped again, placing a hand on the girl's arm. "Maybe it's a dog, Jo. We should have thought of that—there might be guard dogs around this place."

"Oh, great." Jo sounded disgusted. "What do we do now?"

"Let's get back to the party."

They glanced behind them, gauging their escape route.

"Slow . . ." Jo mouthed silently. "Very . . . very . . . slow . . ."

Miranda started to turn around. And then she heard the noise.

A deep, guttural sound from the shrubbery. A low, thick rumbling sound—much, much worse than any dog could ever make.

It was hiding in the shadows where she couldn't see. It made the ground vibrate beneath her feet, and the blood chill in her veins.

"That's not a dog, Jo—" she began, but her voice broke off as the bushes began to tremble.

The girls stared, mesmerized. They watched the branches shake harder, snapping and flailing as something pushed through, as something came purposefully toward them.

Miranda felt Jo's hand gripping her arm. And then she heard Jo's voice—more like a cry, really, as the bushes began to part—

"Oh, God, look at that—"

Miranda saw the eyes.

Huge and yellow, glowing from the blackness of the leaves and shadows, watchful eyes, stealthy eyes, lowering toward the ground now, calmly and boldly assessing them.

The girls stood petrified in terror.

And the tiger crouched, ready to spring.

6

*D*on't move!"

As a voice shouted behind them, the crack of a gunshot shattered the air. To Miranda's horror, the tiger leaped, staggered, then collapsed in a heap on the ground.

"Stay where you are!" the voice shouted again. "Don't touch her!"

Miranda closed her eyes. She could feel her heart hammering in her throat—she could feel the sweat rushing down her forehead. Pressed tight against her, Jo began to tremble. Miranda only hoped her friend wouldn't faint and knock them both down.

Feet were running up now—moving on past the girls and toward the tiger. Miranda opened her eyes and saw someone standing cautiously beside the fallen animal. Even in the gloom she had no trouble recognizing that tall, confident stance. And as Byron

Slater whirled around to face them, Miranda felt all the breath rush out of her in sheer relief.

"You two all right?" he asked worriedly.

Jo took a shaky step forward. "Why'd you have to shoot it? Why—why couldn't you have—"

"She's only stunned," Byron replied. "It's a tranquilizer gun. Nick!" Keeping one eye on the tiger, he cupped his hands around his mouth and shouted again. *"Nick!* Get over here!"

"Did you find her?" a familiar voice yelled back.

The next second Nick crashed through the shrubbery with Harley right on his heels. Both guys stopped and regarded the tiger with anxious frowns.

"Where the hell is Max!" Byron demanded angrily. He flung the gun down on the ground, his face livid. "If I hadn't come along when I did . . ."

"I don't see how—" Nick began, while Harley added, "Max is the only one with a key, so—"

"Fire him," Byron ordered.

The other two eyed each other uneasily.

"Now, come on, Byron," Harley soothed, but Byron cut him off.

"He's through, Harley. I've warned him about checking those cages—*and* about his drinking." His face was set, and his voice lowered dangerously. "There's a party going on, for God's sake. Someone could have been killed."

Again a wary look passed between Nick and Harley. Miranda made a feeble attempt at peacemaking.

"We're really okay," she insisted. "Just a little shaken up, is all."

"Sure," Jo echoed with forced cheerfulness. "We'll be fine."

"Take this young lady back," Byron said quietly, nodding at Jo.

There was an uncomfortable silence. Harley took a step forward as though about to say something, but Byron didn't give him a chance.

"I said, take her back." Byron gave another curt nod in Jo's direction.

"Hey, I'll be glad to take Miranda," Nick volunteered, but Byron waved him away.

"I'll take Miranda. You find Max."

Miranda looked helplessly at Jo, who only shrugged and managed a sly thumbs-up sign while Byron's back was turned. As Harley led Jo away, Nick moved closer to the tiger.

"What are you going to do with her?" Nick asked softly.

"Nothing. This certainly wasn't *her* fault—she was just being true to her nature." Byron knelt in the grass and ran one hand over the creature's sleek head. "Her name's Simba," he explained as Miranda looked on.

"She's your pet?" Miranda asked.

"Sort of. She's part of my zoo."

"You have a zoo?"

"Just a small one."

"I can't believe this." Miranda stared at him, then drew her lips into a tight line. "I can't believe you'd do this to animals."

Byron glanced up at her. "You don't approve?"

"I certainly don't. Animals like this need to be in

their natural habitat, not cooped up in some stupid cage on some stupid estate."

"She's really pretty tame," Nick said helpfully, but Miranda whirled on him.

"Oh, right. That's why she's lying here right now with a tranquilizer dart stuck in her."

Suddenly, more than anything, she wanted to get away. Away from Byron, away from Nick, away from this perfect place where things seemed so unnaturally wrong.

Miranda turned on her heel and started walking, but felt a hand close immediately around her elbow.

"Please don't go."

She stopped. She felt Byron take hold of her other arm and coax her around until she was facing him.

"I shouldn't be here, Byron," she said calmly.

"Of course you should. You won the contest, didn't you?"

"That's not it. What I mean is, I don't *belong* here."

He peered at her intently, that famous face only inches from her own. She saw him give an almost imperceptible nod, and then he murmured, "Let's walk."

"Well, don't mind me!" Nick called after them in exasperation. "I'll just sling this ravenous beast over my shoulder and carry her back to her cage! No problem!"

"Get Max to help you," Byron said matter-of-factly. *"Then* fire him."

He took Miranda's arm and steered her onto a narrow brick pathway she hadn't noticed before.

Then he guided her off through the trees, deeper into the shadows, where the lampposts were fewer and and farther between. They walked quite a while without speaking, and her mind raced in confusion. Where was he taking her, anyway? She shouldn't be out here like this when Jo and Kelly were back at the house, waiting for Byron to show up. At last, in frustration, she blurted out, "Shouldn't you get back to the party?"

Byron didn't break stride. He answered calmly, "I hate parties."

"You hate parties? But—but it's *your* party!"

"It's not my party. It's Peg's party. And Lucille's and Robert's and Zena's party. It's everyone else's party but mine. And since it wasn't my idea to begin with, I don't see why I have to be there."

Miranda hesitated, but then had to smile. "Is that a spoiled-celebrity attitude?"

"I'm not being spoiled, I'm being realistic. I clam up at parties. I can never think of anything intelligent to say."

"No!" Miranda snorted. "Mr. Hero of the big screen who spouts off nearly two whole hours of dialogue in every film! And you can't think of anything to say?"

"Not unless someone writes the lines for me."

He sounded amused at that. Miranda glanced over at his lowered head and saw that he was smiling.

"I'm really sorry about what happened back there," he mumbled. "Simba's getting old and temperamental. Even Max has trouble getting close to her these days."

"Hey, tigers happen."

To Miranda's surprise, Byron laughed. He looked up and laughed, and Miranda thought how nice it sounded, soft and almost shy, as though he hadn't laughed very much in his lifetime and wasn't quite sure he was doing it right.

"So tell me about yourself, Miranda Peterson," Byron said as they continued to walk.

"Is this part of the screening process?" she teased.

"What?"

"You know. Do you take turns with each girl and walk with her in the garden and put her through the third degree?"

"And the wild-animal test. Don't forget that."

"Oh, right. I hope I passed."

"With flying colors."

"Do you like living here?"

His tone was evasive. "Who *wouldn't* like living here?"

"Me. I wouldn't like living here."

"Why not?"

"It's not natural, is it? It's like you've created this whole perfect world for yourself, and everything's so rich and so beautiful, but nothing's real."

"That's what movie stars do," Byron said dryly. "At least, that's what I've been told."

They continued in silence. Then Miranda stopped on the path and faced him squarely.

"You hate it. Don't you?"

Byron peered at her with no expression. For a long moment he stood there without answering, and then finally he gave a faint nod.

"Yes," he mumbled. "I hate it."

Abruptly he turned and started down the path away from her. Miranda hurried to catch up.

"Wait!" she called. "Byron, wait! I'm sorry, I shouldn't have said that! I didn't mean to upset you!"

She saw him slow down. And then she heard a faint buzzing noise, as though a telephone were ringing somewhere close by. To her dismay she watched Byron lift a tiny cellular from his shirt pocket, unfold it, and hold it to his ear.

"What?" he demanded irritably.

She couldn't hear the conversation; she could only watch the lines suddenly strain and tighten on Byron's face. Without a word he folded the telephone and stood stiffly on the path, gazing at her as though he'd never seen her before.

"Byron?" Miranda approached him cautiously. "What is it?"

"Max wasn't drinking," he murmured.

"Max? The one who takes care of the animals?"

"Max . . . wasn't drinking," Byron repeated slowly. "In fact, he's not even here—he went into town. Nick says the keys are hanging in his office, right where they're supposed to be."

"Then how did Simba get out?"

Byron took a step toward her. She could see questions struggling over his face.

"I don't know. Harley's searching the grounds now. But . . ."

His voice trailed off as he stared pensively through the trees.

"What is it?" Miranda asked. "What are you thinking?"

"Whenever I'm home," Byron said softly, "I always walk through the same part of the zoo every evening. To one particular bench near a fountain. It's very private . . . very hidden from everything. I'm always alone there. It's where I meditate."

Miranda shook her head. "I don't understand."

"That's the only reason I noticed Simba's cage was empty. Because I walked right past it." He drew a deep breath. "Do you believe in coincidences, Miranda?"

"Coincidences? I guess that depends on—"

He didn't give her a chance to finish. Without warning he put both hands on her shoulders, staring down at her with smoldering eyes.

"I went away for a while hoping things would get better. I went away because they thought I should, because nobody would believe what I tried to tell them. But now they've *got* to believe me—they've *got* to listen!"

"Byron, please, that hurts—"

"I don't believe in coincidences. I don't believe in them at all."

He stopped then. His voice went even lower, and his fingers dug mercilessly into her skin.

"I think I was supposed to be killed tonight," Byron whispered. "I think Simba was supposed to attack *me.*"

7

For an endless moment all Miranda could do was stare. Stare at the hardness of Byron's face, at the anger and confusion in Byron's eyes.

So I didn't imagine what I heard earlier outside my room. Byron really was upset—he really did say something about being threatened. . . .

Byron's hands slid from her shoulders. He pressed his palms against both sides of his head. He turned away from her and walked a few paces, then lowered his arms to his sides and stared off silently into the darkness.

A wave of compassion rushed over her. What must he be feeling now, she wondered, having shown this vulnerable side of himself to a total stranger? He was probably mortified—he'd want her to leave—he wouldn't want even to look at her again, wouldn't want to be reminded of this little scene here in the garden. . . .

"Damn," Byron mumbled.

He heaved a huge sigh and sat down on the ground. He lowered his head between his hands. Without even thinking, Miranda sat beside him.

Minutes passed. The night pressed heavy upon them, the sweet scent of flowers, the cool caress of fog. They sat that way without speaking for a very long time.

"Well," Byron said at last. "That was a sweet little scene, wasn't it. I'm sure you think I'm perfectly out of my mind." There was no real emotion in his voice now. It was calm and matter-of-fact . . . almost amused, Miranda realized.

"No." Miranda shook her head. "No, I don't."

"That's why they send Byron Slater away on vacations. *Secret* vacations, mind you, so the press won't hear and tag along. Byron Slater's a very private sort of guy, you know. He thinks people are after him; he imagines dangers that aren't there."

"I guess . . ." Miranda hesitated, thought a minute, went on. "I guess I wouldn't believe anything about Byron Slater unless Byron Slater told me it was true."

"Why not? Everyone else around here does."

"I'm not everyone else."

Byron closed his eyes. He tilted his head back, and she thought he might have laughed softly, deep in his throat.

He sighed. "So I guess this means I'm stuck with you."

Miranda regarded him with a puzzled stare. "What do you mean?"

"Well, now that I've confided my deep, dark secret, I guess I'll have to make sure you win the contest, right? To protect my reputation?"

Miranda kept staring. A slow burn of indignation rose up from the pit of her stomach and spread slowly through her body. Without another word she got to her feet and stepped back from him, her hands clenched on her hips.

"You know, in spite of what you think, there are still people in the world who have integrity . . . who have *decency."* The words spilled out before she could stop them, and through a cloud of anger she saw the stunned surprise on Byron's face. "I don't know who you think you are," Miranda rushed on, "but I'm not into blackmail, okay? You can keep your deep, dark secret, *and* your stupid contest, for all I care. There are two other girls back there who'd *much* rather be with you than I would!"

With a last furious glance, Miranda spun on her heel and stomped away. She hadn't expected Nick to be right behind her, and as they collided full force, he nearly fell off the path.

"How long have you been here!" Miranda demanded.

"How long? Me?" Nick sputtered. "Not long—I just got here, as a matter of fact."

"Will you please take me back to the party?" Miranda requested icily.

Nick glanced from her angry expression to Byron, who was still sitting on the ground.

"Uh . . . sure," Nick said, stepping back, putting

a respectful distance between Miranda and himself. "This way."

"Thank you so much."

"Don't mention it."

"And don't ask me what happened."

"Don't worry."

"What a jerk. I should have known! I mean, they're all alike, right? Big egos, lots of money, think they can run the world and all the people in it."

"I have no ego, and I'm very poor. Just in case you're interested."

"I'm not."

"Fine. I *so* admire your honesty."

"How much farther is it?"

"Well, if you just keep on this walkway and follow it as far as it goes, you'll end up at the party."

"Wonderful. You don't need to come with me, then."

"Does this mean I'm dismissed?"

"Thank you for your help, but I'm fine now."

"Yeah, I can see that."

"Goodbye."

Nick stepped off the path, grinned, and made a low-sweeping bow. "And a very nice evening to you, too."

As Miranda came out through the foliage and started toward the terrace, Lucille came running up to meet her.

"Where have you been!" Lucille exclaimed. "I've been looking all over for you! You can't just wander off and not tell anyone where you're going—we have things planned! Peg's been having an absolute fit! You're missing an important photo session!"

Before Miranda could answer, she saw Jo waving at her madly from the other side of the pool. Kelly was standing by a rose arbor, her face posed in an exquisite smile, while a photographer snapped a continuous stream of pictures and a tiny woman swathed in chiffon, a turban, and feathers instructed her which way to move her eyes.

"Ah, there's Zena—she's dying to meet you! Come on!" Lucille insisted, grabbing Miranda's arm and marching her over to the others. "Here she is—I found her!" she shouted while all the chattering groups of people turned with phony smiles. Miranda almost expected them to break into polite applause, and in spite of her anger, it was all she could do to keep from laughing.

"Group shot, I think, Miguel," Lucille directed, pulling Jo one way, Miranda another. When each of them was in position on either side of Kelly, Lucille clapped her hands at the photographer. "Then we'll go for candid shots. Girls partying, girls having fun, girls not posing." She raised an eyebrow at Kelly and added, "We want this to look *natural,* remember— not *premeditated.*"

For a split instant Kelly's perfect smile turned almost frosty. As she quickly recovered her poise, Jo winked at Miranda, and the three of them continued with the shoot.

"Okay, great!" Lucille finally announced. "Go on, you three, relax and have fun! You've earned it!"

Relieved, Miranda and Jo escaped to one of the tables as far from the crowds as possible.

"What happened!" Jo whispered loudly. "I've

been imagining all sorts of things! All wonderful, of course."

"Not so wonderful." Miranda sighed. "He's a total jerk."

"No!"

"Yes. And I lied about you."

"About me?" Jo looked surprised. "What'd you say?"

"I said you'd much rather win the contest than I would."

"You didn't," Jo groaned, then burst out laughing. "Well, I'm sure *that* made quite an impression on Byron Slater. I'm sure *that'll* keep him awake every night this week, trying to decide between me and Kelly!"

"I wish I could go home," Miranda grumbled.

"Well, what did he do that was so jerkish?" Jo persisted. "Did he try . . . uh . . . you know . . ."

"No, nothing like that." Miranda shook her head, frowning.

"Well, what then?"

"Oh, just—"

"Shhh! Here he comes!"

As a ripple of anticipation swept through the party, Miranda saw Byron working his way slowly along one side of the swimming pool. Harley walked behind him, looking anything but inconspicuous, and Miranda noticed how Byron's eyes continuously scanned the crowd.

For one brief instant she felt a twinge of guilt. He was definitely on guard, definitely aware of everything and everyone around him. She could still see the expression on his face back there in the garden,

she could still hear the echo of his voice—
"Someone's trying to kill me." She wished now that
she hadn't gone off in such a huff. She wished now
that she'd encouraged him to open up and tell her
what was going on.

"Just look at Kelly," Jo said in disgust. "She's
hanging all over the poor guy!"

"He doesn't seem to be fighting her off."

"Well, how could he, really, without looking
rude!"

Miranda had to smile at that. As they watched
Kelly drape herself repeatedly over Byron, Harley
nudged the star firmly ahead. *Byron's moving like a
robot,* Miranda thought. *Like someone who's been
programmed to be friendly and polite but isn't really
enjoying it.*

I don't care, Miranda told herself firmly. *I don't
care anything about him or what he's feeling.* And yet
the revelation bothered her, all the same. Nobody
else seemed to notice Byron's hesitancy or his edgi-
ness, but Miranda kept watching his eyes, and how
they darted back and forth, back and forth, over all
those admiring faces.

He is *afraid,* she realized with a shock. *I think he
really is afraid of something.*

"He's looking at you," Jo whispered, and Miranda
snapped back to attention.

"No, he's not."

"He is so. And he's heading this way." Jo paused,
then added smugly, "Much to Kelly's disappointment, I'm sure."

Miranda glanced around for an escape. Jo stepped
purposefully behind her with another smug smile.

"Miranda," Byron said, stopping in front of her, taking her hand in his. Harley positioned himself several inches from Byron and tactfully redirected his gaze out over the crowd. "And Jo," Byron added politely. He fixed both girls with a questioning look, but before he could say anything else, Jo leaned in with a conspiratorial whisper.

"Don't worry. We haven't said anything about the wild marauding beast."

Byron's smile was relieved. As Miranda tried to pull her hand from his grasp, he fixed his eyes levelly on hers.

"I'm sorry," he mumbled. "Not just for Simba. I shouldn't have said what I did."

Miranda didn't know how to respond. Seeing Jo's puzzled expression, she gave Byron a brief nod, then turned around as a voice broke into the awkward silence.

"There you are, Byron. Aren't you going to introduce me to your lovely guests?"

The man standing behind them looked casual and comfortable and totally self-assured, with a slow, easy smile and kind blue eyes. His hands were thrust deep into his pants pockets, and he rocked back a little on his heels, surveying the girls thoughtfully.

"How can I, Robert?" Byron replied, smoothly. "I've just barely met them myself."

Robert lifted an eyebrow, a smile playing at the corners of his lips. "Little slipup there, I admit. Should have called you—let you know what was going on."

"Yes, you should have," Byron replied, though he didn't seem upset about it now. In fact, his tone had lightened considerably, as though sparring with Robert was an old and enjoyable game.

"Miranda and Jo," Byron gave in. "And now I guess you'll just monopolize them the rest of the evening."

"Hi, Miranda—hi, Jo, I'm Robert," the man went on, ignoring Byron completely. "Byron's conscience, confidante, and cohort in crime."

"Nice to meet you," Miranda said. He looked a little older than Byron, and his handshake felt solid and trustworthy. As he and Byron exchanged smiles, she could actually see Byron relaxing in this man's presence.

"So, I hear you girls have quite a full itinerary this week," Robert mused, rocking back on his heels again, staring off calmly through the chattering crowd.

"So why don't you tell *me?*" Byron retorted.

"Okay, let's see. Photo shoots, shopping, dinner at the club . . ." Robert frowned. "Oh, and some fashion-hair-makeup thing I'm not involved in, thank God."

"Sounds exciting," Byron concluded, not sounding excited at all.

"They might be able to visit the set. *If* there's time. And *if* Peg can charm the powers that be." Robert's tone went deadpan. "Even though we all know charm's *never* been one of Peg's greatest assets—"

"It's supposed to be a closed set, anyway," Byron broke in. "I told them I wanted a closed set."

Robert lifted an eyebrow. He opened his mouth as

if to say something, then seemed to change his mind. As Miranda watched, she could almost swear that he and Harley exchanged a quick, secretive look before Robert turned his full attention back to the girls.

"So what else have they planned for you on this trip?" he asked them politely. "Have I left anything out?"

"Only the rest and relaxation part." Jo grunted. "After all this fun, I'm going to be exhausted."

Miranda had to laugh. "We'll have plenty of time to rest," she assured her. "At least that's what Lucille told me."

"Ah, Lucille." Robert winked at Byron. "Now, *she* should be your publicist, if you want my opinion—"

"Yes, Robert." Byron sighed. "I already know your opinion."

"Of course, I'm just your agent—"

"As you keep reminding me—"

"And what do I know about anything—"

"Not very much—"

"And hey, Peg's pushy and rude and has a big mouth, but what does it matter if she rubs people the wrong way? This is only your career we're talking about—"

"I owe Peg," Byron broke in quietly, and Robert stared at him, unruffled.

"You owe her a punch in the face," Robert said.

Behind Byron, Harley ducked his head, putting a hand up to smother a laugh. Even Byron seemed to be having trouble controlling his amusement.

"Yes, well, all right, Robert. You've made your point." He glanced from Miranda to Jo and cleared his throat. "Okay, fine. Moving right along . . . uh, Robert, it *is* time for you to be moving right along, isn't it?"

"I know that tone." Robert nodded, looking quite pleased with himself. "It means I've overstepped my bounds. Again. I can take a hint, Byron, you don't have to hit me over the head with a two-by-four." He stepped back, tipped an invisible hat to them, then wandered off, humming loudly and slightly off-key. The girls watched him go, then burst into laughter.

"Is this what they call dissension among the ranks?" Jo winked at Miranda, while Byron looked slightly embarrassed.

"Sorry about that. Robert's not real good at being subtle."

"Oh, don't worry," Jo assured him in an exaggerated stage whisper. "We're good at keeping secrets, aren't we, Miranda?"

"Would you . . . uh . . . like something to drink?" Byron asked, and Miranda spoke up at once.

"Yes, I'm dying of thirst. Can I get you something?"

Byron gave her a smile. "Hey, that's my line."

"You've got mingling to do," Miranda reminded him, and left him and Jo to talk while she went off in search of the punch bowl.

She'd taken about ten steps when something jolted her from behind.

"Oh, excuse me!" she exclaimed, whirling around. But the waiter already had ahold of her shoulders, trying to steady her.

"My fault," he insisted. "Wasn't watching where I was going."

He was a strange-looking fellow. Broad, squarish shoulders, almost lumpy—long, straggly hair that practically obscured his narrow face—long dark mustache—huge tinted glasses. He was balancing a tray in one hand and immediately reached for a frosted tumbler.

"Here," he said amiably. "Peace offering."

"Thanks a lot. You saved me a trip."

"Go ahead, try it. It's some kind of fancy lemonade."

Miranda did so. "Ummm. That's really good."

"I was looking for Mr. Slater," the waiter told her, and Miranda turned slightly to point.

"He's right over there. I was just getting him something to drink."

"Oh, great! Then would you mind . . . ?" The waiter leaned over, his voice going low. "Would you mind taking this glass over to him? I think it's supposed to be a surprise—at least that's what the bartender told me. Some agent or somebody wants this delivered to him personally."

"Agent?" Miranda asked. "You mean Robert?" She hadn't seen where Robert had gone. Now her glance swept over the party, but he seemed to have disappeared.

"Yeah, whoever," the waiter agreed. "He said give it to Mr. Slater, and don't say who sent it." The waiter straighted up again and laughed. "Some private joke, I guess."

Miranda hesitated, then took the glass in her hand. "Sure, I'd be glad to. Oh, and I need another one for my friend."

"Here you go."

The waiter hurried off, vanishing quickly into the crowd. Miranda stood there a moment staring after him, then shrugged and went back to Jo and Byron.

They were standing just where she'd left them, deeply involved in a discussion about music. She looked down at the three glasses clutched between her hands.

"What took you so long?" Jo teased. "You've been gone practically a whole minute."

"Here," Byron said, taking two of the glasses from her. "Let me help."

"No, wait." Miranda started to reach for the glasses, hesitated, then frowned. She took one of them back, stared at it, then handed it uncertainly to Byron. "Wait," she said again. "Oh, darn, I can't remember now which was which."

Byron looked quizzical. "They all look the same to me."

"Have you noticed?" Jo spoke up. "Kelly's glaring at us. My advice is, keep her far away from the toothpicks and cheese slicers."

"Miranda?" Byron asked. "Is something wrong?"

"Yes. No. Oh, I can't remember," Miranda muttered.

"You can't remember if something's wrong?"

"I can't remember about the glasses! And now I've probably ruined the surprise."

"What surprise?" Jo looked blank. "What are you talking about?"

Before Miranda could stop them, both Byron and Jo tipped up their glasses and took long, deep sips of lemonade. Exactly what Miranda expected, she wasn't sure—an expression of some kind—disgust or shock or amusement—*something*—but when neither of them showed any emotion at all, she shrugged and took a drink from her own glass.

"That hits the spot!" Jo regarded her half-empty glass with a contented sigh. "I could drink at least ten more of these. How about you, Miranda?"

Miranda nodded and took another sip.

And it was strange, she thought vaguely, how Byron's lips seemed to be moving, but there were no words coming out. And how the swimming pool suddenly looked like a huge pool of thick, black ink . . . and how all the lanterns seemed to be exploding, with orange and yellow sparkles shimmering over everyone's faces . . .

"—all right?" she heard someone say, and *Who is that?* she wondered. *Who is that talking to me so far away . . . ?*

"—all right, Miranda?" the voice said again. *Yes, I know that voice, that's Byron's voice, Byron Slater the movie star,* only it was muffled and fading, just as Byron's dark eyes were fading, just as everything around her was fading now, and she felt as if she were sliding away, trying so hard to pay attention but falling down instead—

"—Miranda!" the voice shouted, but she couldn't answer, she couldn't do anything, except grope out and try to hang on to her glass.

It fell from her fingers.

It fell in slow motion, catching the sparkles of light, and then she was falling, too, down . . . down . . . onto the stones of the terrace.

8

She fainted, that's all. There's no need to make a big deal out of it, Byron. Fans *have* been known to faint in the presence of big stars. It's not unusual, and it's certainly no cause for alarm."

"She didn't faint, Peg."

"Really? Sure *looks* like a faint."

"What I mean is, she didn't faint because of *me.*"

Byron . . . Byron Slater . . . I'd know that voice anywhere.

"And I don't know why you had to bring her in here. Nobody should be using this room, Byron. This room should be private and strictly off limits."

"Thank you so much, Peg. I'll certainly take that under advisement."

"You don't have to get sarcastic."

"You don't have to stay."

Byron Slater. That's right. I'm spending the week

at Byron Slater's estate, and that's him talking right now. . . .

Miranda struggled to wake up. She felt as if she were underwater, fighting to get to the surface, but her body was weighted down, clumsy and sluggish, and all she could do was thrash helplessly in place.

An image of Byron's face flashed through her mind.

An image of Byron's face, and then another face, as well—one with tinted eyeglasses and a mustache and wisps of straggly hair—

"The waiter," Miranda mumbled.

She sat up at last, and her eyes flew open.

At first everything swam around her in a hazy light, but then, slowly, she realized that *people* were standing around her, bending over her, all of them looking grave and concerned.

"Miranda, thank God." Byron breathed a sigh of relief and sat down beside her. "Are you all right?"

"It was the waiter," Miranda mumbled. She wanted to speak up, but her words were all soft and slurred. "Waiter," she tried again.

"What'd she say?" Peg sounded almost angry, and Byron frowned, straining to hear.

"Water," he told Peg. "She said she'd like some water."

"No," Miranda whispered, but Byron pushed her gently back into the cushions of the couch.

"So what are you saying, Byron?" Peg demanded, coming back again, shoving a glass of water beneath Miranda's nose. "Are you saying something was wrong with her drink? Are you saying someone's after the guests now? What'll it be next? Should we frisk the meter reader when he shows up? Maybe fingerprint the plumber before he comes to fix the toilet?"

Byron took the glass from her and said carefully, "I'm just saying I'd like to know why she fainted, that's all—"

"Well, I know what you're *thinking*, Byron, and it's totally out of the question," Peg said. *"Totally* out of the question."

Robert's head suddenly appeared over Byron's shoulder. "I don't think this is anything we need to discuss right now, do you, Peg? After all, Miranda would probably like to rest a little so she can get back to the party."

Peg walked stiffly to the door, and Robert followed her out. But as they disappeared into the hallway, Miranda could still hear Peg's voice, loud and clear.

"You know how important this publicity is, Robert! How hard I've worked! How these girls have their hearts set on spending a week with Byron! If you ask me to call it off, we won't be able to hold our heads up! There'll be questions and speculations and outright lies—we'll be sued—we'll be shunned—we'll be laughed at—"

"Let me worry about that, Peg," Robert replied calmly. "Just go on back to the party and charm everyone. It's what you do best."

Byron gave a halfhearted smile. Miranda heard the door shut, and then Robert rejoined them, one hand thrust deep in a pocket, the other scratching thoughtfully at his chin.

"Byron, you know I'd rather have my skin scraped

off with iron combs than ever agree with Peg." He sighed. "However—"

"I know, I know, she has a point," Byron cut him off. "And you can talk in front of Miranda—I've already told her I'm in danger."

Robert's face registered no expression. For an endless moment he gazed down at Byron, then finally let out a long sigh.

"That's really great, Byron. I'm sure this is *just* what she wanted to hear at the start of her dream week."

"It doesn't matter," Byron replied. "She doesn't believe me, anyway."

"He *is* crazy, you know," Robert pointed out. "It's something we try to keep hidden from the press, but the guy is really and truly out of his mind." He walked a few paces, stopped, then turned back to face them. "This is probably none of my business, Byron, but exactly *why* did you choose to share your feelings of paranoia with this young lady?"

Byron glanced at Miranda, then back to Robert. "I like her."

"Ah." Robert nodded.

"Oh, please," Miranda groaned, sitting up again. "Look, Byron, this isn't a movie we're in, okay? So don't feed me one of your lines and expect me to think it's real."

"See?" Byron's eyes met Robert's, and he shrugged. "I told you."

Robert gazed down at the floor. He rocked back on his heels several times, then lifted his head, peered at Byron, and nodded again.

Okay," he said. "I like her, too. So what do we do now?"

Miranda opened her mouth, then closed it again. She felt so sleepy . . . almost as if she were floating, and yet she could see the sharp, tight lines of Byron's face, the sad concern in Robert's eyes as he stared at Byron. She remembered Byron's reaction earlier in the garden, the things he'd said to her. She glanced down and saw his hand resting lightly on her arm.

"The waiter." She spoke more clearly this time. "There was a waiter, and he asked me to bring you a glass of lemonade."

Now she had their attention. Both Byron and Robert were watching her with puzzled expressions.

"He handed me this glass. . . ." Miranda went on. "He said your agent had asked the bartender to give it to you."

"My agent?" Byron cast a sidelong glance at Robert, who merely shrugged and looked blank.

"He said . . ." Miranda's mind was feather-light. She tried hard to think. "He said 'some agent' . . . He said 'some agent or somebody.'"

"What does that mean?"

"Anyone who works for you, is my guess," Robert concluded.

"I thought he meant you," Miranda admitted guiltily, and Robert looked startled.

"Me? Why?"

"When he said agent, I asked if it was you. I said your name."

"And he *said* it was Robert?" Byron persisted.

Miranda shook her head. "Not exactly. I guess I

just assumed he said yes. But now that I think about
it . . ."

"You gave him an answer, and he grabbed it,"
Byron concluded.

Miranda's eyes drifted shut. She forced them open
once more.

"He thought it was supposed to be a surprise," she
added. "Then I got the glasses mixed up, and I
couldn't remember which was which. You and Jo
each took one . . . I drank the one that was left."

"So," Byron said slowly, "you probably got the
one meant for me."

Robert shook his head. "Byron—" he began, but
Miranda groped for Byron's hand.

"He might have been wearing a disguise," she
murmured. "His shoulders were sort of lumpy . . .
like padding. His hair didn't look real."

"Byron—" Robert tried again, but this time it was
Byron who interrupted.

"Was everyone screened when they came in?"

"Everyone," Robert said firmly.

"Are you sure?"

"Of course I'm sure—"

"Well, can we find that waiter and check him out
again?"

"Byron, wait. Listen to me, will you please?"

As Byron went silent, Robert refocused his attention on Miranda.

"You said the waiter *assumed* it was supposed to
be a surprise? Not that someone actually *said* it was
a surprise?"

Miranda managed a nod.

"Then I think there's a logical explanation," Robert said quietly.

Miranda squinted, narrowing in on Robert's eyes. She saw the calm reassurance there . . . and then, suddenly, something else she hadn't noticed before. *Pity?* Was that *pity* she saw there, just behind the compassion? Pity for who? *Byron?*

"Someone probably *did* send that waiter over," Robert went on gently. "Think about it, Byron. It could have been Walt."

Byron stared at him. Miranda saw a muscle clench in his jaw, and then slowly, slowly he stood up.

"Walt," he echoed. "So . . . what exactly are you telling me, Robert?"

Robert was beginning to look a little uncomfortable, Miranda thought. "Come on, Byron." He held out both hands in an appeasing gesture. "I didn't have anything to do with this. And in all fairness to Walt, if you'd just cooperate, he wouldn't have to resort to things like this—"

"I don't want to hear it." Byron cut him off, staring straight into Robert's eyes. "Not a word, okay? It was a *stupid* thing to do."

"Yes." Robert sighed. "I agree."

"And Miranda drank it by mistake." Byron's tone was hard and unforgiving. "She could sue us, Robert—no—she *should* sue us! Good God, are there any *other* little secrets you'd like to let me in on before somebody else gets hurt?"

Robert shook his head. "No. And I'm sorry. This should never have happened."

"Where is he?" Byron demanded.

"I'm not sure," Robert hedged. "But, Byron, can't this wait till—"

"No, it can't wait. You stay here with Miranda in case she needs anything."

In total dismay Miranda watched as Byron stormed out. Robert moved closer to the couch, folding his arms over his chest, regarding her with a solemn frown.

What's going on? I'm so sleepy, and nothing's making any sense. . . .

Miranda's eyes drooped shut. She forced them open again as Robert cleared his throat.

"If Byron says he likes you, then I believe him," he said matter-of-factly. "For whatever reason, when Byron makes up his mind about something, it's that simple—he's made up his mind."

Miranda's lips opened in surprise. Her mind groped for something to say, but Robert calmly went on.

"And since Byron's decided to take you into his confidence, Miranda, I think there's something you should know." Robert paused then. He shifted his feet and stared down at the carpet, his voice troubled. "Byron's been under a lot of strain lately. Too much work . . . too tight a schedule . . . not enough rest. When you're as famous as he is, the world watches your every move, and Byron's *intensely* private—which is not exactly the way to survive in this business. Right now he's supposed to be on medication—which he conveniently forgets to take—and so Walt—his doctor—has to sneak it in wherever he can."

Again he hesitated, almost guiltily, Miranda thought.

"Like lemonade, for instance," Robert clarified. "Walt's *probably* the one who asked that waiter to take the drink over. The one *you* drank instead of Byron. It's nothing to be worried about. Still . . . sedatives work differently on different people. And this one *is* a little strong."

"So . . ." Miranda's mind was drifting again, thoughts confused and blurry. "So . . . what are you saying?"

"What I'm saying," Robert continued slowly, "is that we'd all really appreciate it if you wouldn't mention this little incident to anyone else."

"No," she murmured. "No . . . of course I won't."

"You know how rumors get started—and Byron hates rumors. He's supposed to start shooting his new film right away, and he doesn't need any more pressures."

Miranda nodded. She really wished Robert would leave so she could sleep again. She was trying so hard to keep her mind clear . . . her eyes open . . .

"He shouldn't have problems in his life right now," Robert said quietly. "He can't afford complications. And our job is to keep those problems away from him. You understand that. Don't you, Miranda?"

He smiled down at her.

Then he walked slowly into the hall and closed the door behind him.

9

Why did he tell me all that stuff about Byron?

Miranda lay there, staring hazily up at the ceiling. *Personal stuff . . . private stuff about Byron. Why?* She was just some unknown, unimportant person who'd happened to win a contest in a magazine—certainly not anyone some big star would ever confide in.

But *"he likes you,"* Robert had said. *"If Byron Slater says he likes you, then I believe him."*

This is definitely weird, she thought groggily. *Like being in a bad movie with no plot and a bunch of characters who don't make any sense.*

She wished again that she could go home. She wished she could just pick up the phone right now and call Amy, but Amy was away counseling at summer camp, and almost impossible to reach. Most of all she wished she hadn't made such a fool of herself at the party, falling down like some stupid rag doll. She imagined *that* had made Kelly very happy, and that Jo was probably wondering where she'd gone. Then she drifted off into sleep.

When she woke again, everything was still. The room was dark, save for one lamp near the door, and Miranda sat up slowly, rubbing her head. She could see now that it was a den or study of some kind, quite large, with built-in bookshelves and elegantly framed posters from Byron's films. The shelves were full of trophies and figurines; the other two walls held plaques, photographs, and various framed items. *Awards,* she realized suddenly. *These must all belong to Byron.*

She walked over to one of the shelves . . . ran a finger gingerly over a statuette. And what must it feel like, she wondered, to have a whole room set aside just for your achievements, just for all the different testimonies to your fame and success? She couldn't begin to imagine. She continued on around the room, finally stopping at a large mahogany desk. Its surface was cluttered with papers and file folders, magazines and books, several Rolodexes, some hastily scribbled memos, and baskets overflowing with mail.

Miranda started to pick up one of the notes, then stopped herself. *What are you doing—this isn't any of your business!* Yet she couldn't help but be curious, and so she riffled through a top layer of papers. They were all the same—neatly typed messages of appreciation, with the handwritten name "Byron Slater" stamped at the bottom of each one.

Form letters, she realized. Personal replies to Byron Slater's fans. Answers to the hundreds and thousands of letters he received every day—loving, adoring letters he would probably never read, from girls he would probably never know.

The thought made her sad somehow—sad and disillusioned. She put the papers back in place and began browsing through the rest of the clutter.

A pocket dictionary. A dog-eared copy of *Catcher in the Rye. The Greatest Movies Ever Made.* Issues of *Premiere, Movieline, Film Comment,* and *People.* A long-outdated *TV Guide.* A photo album stuffed with loose pictures. A copy of *Entertainment Weekly* with Byron's smiling face on the cover. A rolled-up edition of *USA Today.*

Curious, Miranda opened the magazine with Byron's picture, scanning through it till she found the corresponding article. The feature raved about the actor and his talents, but bemoaned the fact that his last two movies hadn't done nearly as well at the box office as expected. Spokespersons for the star blamed everything on "unavoidable problems on the set"—citing strong personality differences between the star, various directors, scriptwriters, and even difficult crew members. The article ended with high hopes for Byron's next film—another action-packed adventure with "plenty of thrills and sizzling romance."

Miranda had to smile. There was no getting around it—of the three contestants, Kelly was definitely the only one who had potential for sizzling, both on screen *and* off.

Still laughing to herself, Miranda closed the magazine. She hadn't noticed how one particularly tall stack of mail had begun to tip over, and now, as she straightened up, a whole flood of papers and envelopes slid off the desk and onto the floor, taking the newspaper and several magazines with it.

Oh, great, Miranda, look what you've done now.

Quickly she knelt down and began gathering everything up, keeping one eye to the door. It'd be just her luck for someone to come in and find her snooping. She threw several handfuls of stuff onto the desk and was just retrieving the rolled-up copy of *USA Today* when the newspaper suddenly popped open, spilling something out beside her foot.

Miranda leaned over, staring at it with a frown.

An autograph book?

Intrigued, she leaned closer. It sure *looked* like an autograph book, lying open where it had fallen. She could see that several lines had been scrawled across the two facing pages, and the thick letters spread out in a curious reddish-brown stain.

Like blood . . .

Miranda's lips parted soundlessly. She drew back a little, shaking her head.

The writing *did* look like blood, she thought with a start—*dried* blood—smeared across the paper and left to dry. . . .

"I think I was supposed to be killed tonight. . . ."

Byron's words came back to her again, and Miranda tried to block them from her mind. *Quit letting your imagination get the best of you!* Cautiously she leaned in for another look, squinting down at the pages, trying to read the blurred handwriting.

STARSTRUCK

And then, as the message became clear, she felt a cold uneasiness creep through her.

TO BYRON FROM YOUR STARSTRUCK FAN—
IF I CAN'T HAVE YOU,
NO ONE CAN.

10

Miranda stared at the book.

She read the message through again, and then she pulled out a chair and sat down at the desk.

It's just a message, for God's sake, just a stupid message in a stupid autograph book. It certainly wasn't anything to get upset about, she told herself firmly—and yet she couldn't shake the queasy feeling building inside of her, the feeling that something was very wrong. . . .

She flipped through the rest of the pages. To her surprise, all of them were blank.

Miranda propped her elbows on the desk, rested her chin between her hands. She didn't hear the door opening behind her, or the footsteps approaching stealthily across the carpet. She didn't hear anything at all, until the hand came down on her shoulder, causing her to jump up with a scream.

"Miranda!" Byron stepped back. "Calm down, it's just me. I came back to see how you're doing."

Shaken, Miranda stared at him. He looked so handsome—even more handsome than the last time, if that was possible—his chiseled features bathed in the lampglow, his eyes so dark, so intense. She lowered her head self-consciously and managed to stammer, "I'm—I'm fine. Much better, in fact."

"What's wrong? You look like you've seen a ghost."

"I . . ." Her eyes moved briefly toward the desk. *I can't tell him what I was thinking. . . . If I tell him, I'll look like a total idiot.* "I . . ." Miranda tried again, shrugging her shoulders helplessly.

"I'm afraid it's going to be one of those parties," Byron went on dryly. "You know . . . the kind that never ends?"

Miranda nodded.

"Well . . . do you want to go back?" he asked her. "Or go up to bed? Or . . ." This time it was Byron who shrugged his shoulders. "Or *what?*"

Miranda shook her head.

"Why are you staring at me like that?" Byron asked her uneasily.

Miranda averted her eyes. She managed a soft laugh.

"Sorry, I didn't mean to. Wow—I was just admiring all these awards. Yours, right? And all the fan mail and everything . . ."

Byron barely glanced at the desk. "That's only a very small part of the fan mail. Stuff my office thinks deserves personal attention." He actually looked sheepish. "I don't even see most of it, to tell you the truth. Not that I wouldn't like to—it's just that I wouldn't have time for anything else if I tried to go through it all."

"I bet."

Byron paused, then reached out for her, pulling her close. "Miranda, what *is* it? Did something else happen while you were in here?"

"Why?" Miranda gazed up at him, frowning. "Why would you ask me that?"

"I don't know. You just act like something's wrong, that's all."

"I do?" Again her eyes shifted to the desk, to the autograph book lying there in plain, awful sight. She shut her eyes, opened them again, and let out a sigh. "Okay, look, at the risk of losing what's left of my credibility, I saw something over here, and it upset me a little, that's all."

Byron stared at her, looking completely baffled. "What are you talking about? *What* did you see?"

"Well . . . this autograph book. It fell off the desk, and I picked it up."

"Autograph book? What autograph book?"

Byron followed her pointing finger. Miranda saw the brief flash of curiosity on his face as he reached over and pulled the book into the light. She saw his eyes sweep over the pages. She saw his body begin to stiffen . . . his expression go stony . . . his jaw clamp into place.

"Where'd this come from?" Byron asked quietly.

"I told you, it fell off the desk and—"

"I know that, but *where* did it come from? Where did it *fall* from?"

"It was inside the paper. The rolled-up newspaper." She made a vague gesture with her hand. "I put everything right here."

Quickly Byron went through the pile on the desktop. "Has anyone come in since you've been here?"

Now it was Miranda's turn to look bewildered. "I don't think so. Unless they came in while I was asleep. Why—"

"Shhh!" Holding a finger to his lips, he moved silently to the door and pushed it shut. Then he returned to Miranda's side, shaking his head at her in warning.

"Promise me," he said. "I don't want you telling anyone else about this. At least not now."

Miranda gave a slow nod. "Yes, I promise. So . . . this *is* something to be concerned about?"

For a long moment Byron said nothing. He paced back and forth between the desk and the window, then stopped with his back to her, gazing out into the night. The silence stretched endlessly. It was Miranda who finally broke it.

"Byron . . ." Miranda took a cautious step toward him. "Look, I know this is none of my business—I mean, you don't even know me, and we've kind of been thrown together with all these weird things happening. But you really look as if you could use a friend, and I'd really like to help if I can. So maybe . . . but only if you *want* to . . . you could tell me what's going on."

She thought he might have laughed. His shoulders moved in a weary shrug.

"Someone's after me, Miranda. It's that simple."

Richie Tankersley Cusick

"Trying . . . to kill you?"

"Yes. Only I have a feeling this person's not going to do it right away. I think she wants it to be a kind of game. To play with me at first . . . to make me afraid. To show me how clever and powerful she is."

"God, Byron, how can you be so sure? Because of the tiger? That really *could* have been an accident, couldn't it? I mean, maybe the lock just broke for some reason—"

"No, not just because of Simba. Because of this book. And . . . other things."

He turned, regarding her with a humorless smile. She sat down and waited for him to go on.

"About a month ago I started feeling like I was being followed," Byron began. "You know how it is when you feel someone watching you—when you feel eyes staring at the back of your head?"

Miranda gave a slow nod.

"I'm not *totally* surrendering to my success yet," Byron went on with a frown. "I still go out on my own whenever I can—or at least I *did*. But then suddenly I started feeling like somebody was with me all the time, hiding, spying on me and watching everything I was doing. At the store, out to dinner, driving my car—sometimes even on the set."

"But everyone has to be checked out when you're filming, right?"

Byron shrugged again. "You'd be surprised how much can slip by. You've got cast and crew there, all the extras, the media and fans around watching— it'd be impossible to keep track of everyone."

"What about Italy? Did you feel like you were being watched while you were there?"

"No. The place I stayed was very private . . . very secluded. And to tell you the truth, it was great. I didn't see anyone, and nobody saw me. I actually got some sleep. It was the first time I felt really safe."

"So you feel threatened by this person," Miranda concluded. "You don't think it could just be curiosity? Some fan just following you for fun? Or what about those obnoxious photographers I'm always hearing about?"

"Paparazzi? No." Byron shook his head and turned back to the window. "No, it's much more serious than that."

"You sound pretty convinced."

"I am."

He parted the curtains a little more. Moonlight shone down through trees, revealing a wide sweeping lawn and illuminated tennis courts in the distance.

"There've been two strange phone calls," Byron went on. "And I know they both came from the same person."

"How do you know?"

"The first one happened really late one night— about three in the morning. I was asleep, and the only reason I answered at all is because it's my private number. At that hour I figured something might be wrong at home with my family."

"But it wasn't them?"

"It was a weird voice—nobody I recognized. But later, when I thought more about it, I was pretty sure it was disguised. It didn't sound normal. It was deep and whispery and kind of muffled."

"A woman?"

"Definitely."

"What'd she say?"

"My name, at first. It took me a couple of minutes to wake up, and I could hear this voice saying my name over and over again. Then I asked who it was, and she said, "I'm starstruck. I'm the one who really loves you."

Miranda stared at him. A slow chill worked up her spine, and she suppressed a shiver.

"What else?" she asked.

"That was it; she hung up."

"Well . . . it sounds innocent enough. Like it could have come from any fan who—"

"No," Byron interrupted. "There was something about that voice. It made me feel really strange and . . . and *cold* inside. And the way she said 'star-struck.'"

"What do you mean?"

"Not like a word just describing herself. It was more like she was telling me her *name.* Like you'd say, 'I'm Miranda.'"

Miranda pondered this a moment. "Then what'd you do?"

"I rang Harley right away. Just to be safe, he had the grounds searched, but they never found any-body. So then I did the only thing I *could* do—had my number changed."

"Has she called back?"

Byron nodded. "I thought maybe it'd end there, that it was just one of those freaky things. Some-times your number gets out, no matter how careful

you are. And you can't live your life being afraid to answer the phone."

He glanced back at her over his shoulder. Miranda managed a weak smile.

"No," she agreed, "I guess you can't."

"Then two days before I left for Italy, I was out by myself, having lunch in a café."

"Should you be doing that?"

"I can't stand it, not having any privacy." Byron sounded defensive. "And you'd be surprised how many people don't even recognize me when I'm alone. I had sunglasses on, and some funky old clothes, and I hadn't shaved in a while."

He halfway grinned at the memory, and Miranda smiled back.

"I was sitting there eating when the cashier came over and said she had a message for me. She said some girl had called and told her it was important."

Byron paused. He made a derisive sound in his throat.

"I could tell the cashier was kind of put out. She handed me this napkin where she'd written down the message. It said, 'Forsake all others or be starstruck.'"

"Meaning . . . she might do something to you?"

Byron shrugged. "That'd be my guess."

"It couldn't have been a mistake?" Miranda asked anxiously. "Somebody calling for some other person?"

"Whoever called described exactly what I was wearing and told the cashier I was at the table in the corner."

"So that means she could see you! She must have been close by!"

"I thought of that, too. I ran out to the sidewalk, but there were so many people on the street. She could have been standing right in front of me, and I wouldn't have known."

Byron turned back in Miranda's direction. His expression was grave.

"I asked the cashier if the girl had left her name, but she said no."

"Could she describe her voice?"

Byron made a vague gesture with his hands. "She said she had trouble understanding her because she talked so low."

"Could the cashier have gotten the message wrong?"

Byron shook his head. "I know it was the same person, Miranda. I *know* it." He walked over to her chair, hesitated, then gazed solemnly down at her. "The thing is, it really doesn't matter *what* I think, because nobody around here seems to believe me. Since there's no real evidence, they're not taking it that seriously. Besides, Peg doesn't want any of this leaking out. Bad press, you know."

"But—but that's terrible!" Miranda sputtered. "I mean, you're paying these people, right? They should *listen* to you!"

Byron almost smiled at that. He walked a few paces and ran one hand back through his hair.

"They prefer to say I'm *overreacting*. That *everyone* gets a few crazy calls in this business. That I'm letting it get to me because I've been *working* too hard. That I'm *stressed*. That I'm *run down*."

"But now you have proof!" Miranda reminded him, pointing to the book. "You can show them this, and they'll *have* to believe you!"

Byron gave a hesitant nod. "And suppose Peg's right? Suppose all this *does* get out to the media, and *they* think I'm crazy, too?"

"No one's going to think that," Miranda assured him gently. "People don't like to see their heroes or their role models being hurt. It makes them sympathetic and—and—*angry*. More loyal, even. I know I'd be furious about it. I *am* furious about it."

She paused, trying to put her thoughts into words. She gazed solemnly into Byron's eyes.

"It's like . . . stars give so much of themselves to the public. So when somebody out there tries to destroy that goodness . . ."

Byron laughed softly. "Hold it. Just a few hours ago you were telling me what a jerk I was. So just for the record, let me remind you I'm *not* that good. Of a person *or* an actor."

Miranda's cheeks flushed. "Well . . . I'm just trying to make a point."

"Point taken." Byron smiled. "With gratitude and humility."

"You're welcome," Miranda murmured.

She watched as he walked to the desk, as he sorted restlessly through the clutter, as though trying to organize his own thoughts. She glanced again at the book and walked up behind him.

"Why didn't anyone find that book?" she asked him. "Doesn't someone check your mail?"

Byron shrugged. "Usually, but not always. It depends on who picks it up. Anyway, I doubt if anyone would have thought to look down in the plastic bag the paper came in. I wouldn't have thought of it, would you?"

"But someone had to put it there. Starstruck—is that what we're calling her? Starstruck—"

"We're?" Byron looked up with a faint smile, and Miranda blushed.

"Well, what I meant was—"

"No, I like the sound of that." Still smiling, he turned his attention back to the desk. "Yes. Starstruck. That's what *we're* calling her."

"Okay. Starstruck had to watch for your paper to be delivered, and then she had to get ahold of it and drop the book inside."

"Anything could have happened, Miranda. She could have dropped the paper off herself, with the book already in it. For that matter, she could have thrown it over the fence and one of the staff picked it up and brought it in. It wouldn't be that hard to get a newspaper into this place. And it always comes to this room first—I'm always the first one to read it. Unless I'm gone, of course."

"Unless you're gone," Miranda repeated slowly. "So that means she knew you were going to be here. She knew you were back from Italy."

Byron paused. His head turned, and he gave Miranda a puzzled frown.

"Wait a minute. What are you saying?"

"There are lots of strangers staying here this week, right?" Miranda asked urgently. "A lot of people you don't know?"

"That's not unusual—I'm always the last to find out *anything* in this place." Then, at Miranda's grave look, Byron added, "Well, sure, but there're always a lot of weird people hanging around that I didn't invite."

"Then maybe she's here."

"What!"

"Maybe Starstruck is here, Byron. Right now—somewhere in this house!"

11

For an endless moment Byron stared at her. At last he turned around, and his hands came down slowly upon her shoulders.

"You mean . . ." He shook his head. The silence was so thick, Miranda could almost hear it, pounding in her brain. "You mean one of the guests?" Byron tried again. "Or . . . or someone working for me?"

She felt sorry for him, then. He looked so stricken, so totally shocked, that she was beginning to wish she hadn't said anything at all.

"Or maybe one of your friends," she went on tentatively. "Maybe they're just trying to play a joke on you. Or like you said before, maybe it's a game to them. You know. Because you're always finding clues and solving mysteries and going after the bad guys in your movies. Maybe they're waiting to see how long it'll take you to figure it out."

Byron released her. He walked to the window and pressed his palms flat against the glass.

"That would be easy, wouldn't it?" His voice was almost wistful. "Turning this whole thing into a movie script? But somehow . . . I still think it's a lot more serious than that."

For several minutes he didn't speak. He gazed out at the darkness, and then his shoulders heaved in a sigh.

"Someone here? Someone I might know? Look, Miranda, I admit I'm no angel, but I can't think of a single thing I've ever done in my whole life that anybody would want to kill me for."

Listening to him, Miranda's heart sank. "Oh, God, Byron, I'm so sorry. I don't even know why I said that. I *shouldn't* have said that. I guess I just got a little carried away, trying to figure things out. I didn't mean—"

"No, *I'm* sorry." He turned then and came back to her, taking her hands in his, peering intently into her eyes. "I know you're only trying to help, and believe me, I appreciate it. This sort of thing has never happened to me before—I don't have the first idea how to handle it. It's so damn frustrating—so damn scary! And I'm not *supposed* to be scared, you know? I mean, it's the kind of stuff I'd expect to happen to *big* stars . . . but not to me."

Miranda gave him an uncertain frown. "Byron, don't you really have any idea how big you *are*? What a huge success you are? How you're known— and admired—all over the world?"

He seemed uncomfortable at her words . . . almost embarrassed. He let go of her hands and moved over to the desk, leaning back against it, folding his arms across his chest.

"All I know is, someone's out there. That she seems to know all about me and where I go and what I do. And it's not just wondering *who* it is—but *why* she's doing it. Why does she want to hurt me?"

"Byron—"

He held up a hand and shook his head. "No, let me finish. When something like this happens, it makes you start thinking—does someone really want me dead? Are they really going to kill me? And when are they going to do it—and how? And then, pretty soon, you don't have a life anymore. Because success takes such a huge part of it away from you, anyway . . . and now this constant worrying—this awful fear—takes away the rest of it."

Miranda couldn't answer. She gazed at the floor and fought back angry tears.

"You could go to the police," she suggested at last. "You're not the first celebrity this has happened to. They'd believe you, wouldn't they?"

"Do you know how many calls these cops get every day from people being harassed and stalked and threatened? And I'm one of the *lucky* ones, Miranda—I'm surrounded by people I *trust,* people who care about my welfare." He hesitated, his brow creased in thought. "I can vouch for my personal staff, Miranda," he insisted again. "We don't always agree, and we don't always get along, but none of them would ever hurt me."

He pulled himself to his full height. He put a hand to his forehead and gently massaged his temple.

"As for the others," he mumbled. "All those other people here . . ."

His voice trailed away. Miranda suddenly realized how exhausted he sounded, and she watched him with growing concern.

"Maybe you're right." He sighed. "Maybe Starstruck *is* here. Maybe she's close to me, and I don't even know it."

"Still, that's pretty unlikely," Miranda said with forced confidence. "I mean, I really don't see how it could happen, when you think about it. Everyone has to be checked out before Harley lets them in. And even if *you* don't know a lot of these people, *somebody* knows them, or they wouldn't be here."

Byron gave a vague nod. "Yes, you're right. It makes sense, doesn't it. Nobody could get to me here. I'm really very safe."

Yet his voice seemed almost distant now. And he didn't sound angry anymore, or even frightened, Miranda thought to herself—it was more a calm sort of . . . what? Resignation?

Maybe he is tired. We've spent way too much time on this.

"And don't forget your lifeline," she heard herself saying. "It shows you're going to be around for a long time."

Byron showed no response. Miranda crossed slowly to his side, watching as his eyes finally lifted and focused on her.

"What?" he mumbled.

"Your lifeline," Miranda repeated, more insistently. "I told you—it means you're going to live to be really old."

At last her words seemed to register. She could see a faint smile playing at the corners of his mouth, and he bent his head to look down at her.

"I need a friend, Miranda," he said gravely. "Is that you?"

His look held her. She felt the strong pull of his eyes and saw his face lower again toward hers.

"Byron!" Startled, Miranda glanced toward the door. "Did you hear something?"

"What?"

"Something!" she whispered. "A noise? Like maybe someone started to come in just now?"

Byron immediately stepped in front of her. Motioning her to keep still, he crossed the room and pressed his ear against the doorframe. With one quick movement he had the door open and was out in the hallway, returning a moment later, shaking his head.

"Empty. Nobody there."

They stared at each other. Miranda felt goose bumps prickling over her arms.

"But someone *was* there," she said softly. "I'm sure of it."

12

What happened to you last night, Miranda?"

Lucille came into the bedroom and stood with her hands on her hips, brows drawn into a worried frown. From a soft nest of pillows, Miranda gave a languorous stretch and smiled up at her.

"Are you feeling better?" Lucille went on. "One minute you were there at the party, and then I realized you weren't! And when I asked about you, Peg said you'd gotten sick and gone to bed!"

"Too much excitement, I guess," Miranda said evasively. "Did you have a good time?"

"Of course I had a good time—I always have a good time. Did *you* have a good time? What little time you were there?"

"Today will be better," Miranda hedged again and threw back the covers. "Is that sunshine I see behind those curtains?"

"It's a glorious day," Lucille agreed, stepping over to the French doors, throwing them wide to the morning air. "Ummm . . . smell those roses! Well, I guess even roses are easy to grow when you have professional gardeners all over the place." She turned back and let out a whistle. "Wow! Where did you get those fancy pajamas?"

"It was the strangest thing," Miranda explained. "When I got back to my room last night, a maid came in and wanted to take all my measurements. Then, when I got out of the shower later, someone had left these pajamas on my bed." Miranda ran her hand over the silky fabric. "Nice, huh?"

"I'll say. I'm sure Zena was behind all that. I told her about your suitcase, and she promised you'd have clothes to wear in the meantime. She's got *ultra* taste, if you know what I mean. She'll be going with you on your shopping spree."

"Well, whoever it was also left a toothbrush, a hairbrush, and some clean underwear." Miranda pointed to the lacy lingerie laid out on a chair. "Have you ever seen anything so delicate?"

"It's so you," Lucille teased, and Miranda gave her an impish smile.

"I think I could get used to this."

"Who couldn't? Wish I'd lost *my* suitcase."

"Did anyone miss me at the party last night?" Miranda chuckled. "Did Kelly ask where I was?"

"Actually, Jo was pretty upset," Lucille replied. "And lonely, too, I think. I'm glad you two seem to get along so well—she's a nice girl." Lucille paused and rolled her eyes. "As for Kelly—she wasn't what I'd call overly concerned about you, no. In fact, she's the hottest topic of everyone's conversation. She's certainly not trying to hide what *she* wants from Byron."

Miranda grinned. "Well, I'm sure he can't help but notice her."

"And how about you?"

"How *about* me?"

"What do you think of Byron Slater? Any comments? Ideas? Suggestions?"

Miranda walked out onto the balcony. "He's nice," she replied. "Just like you said."

"I think he's pretty taken with you," Lucille mused, coming up behind her. "At least, that seems to be the general opinion of those in the know. Good Lord, what on earth is that?"

Clutching Miranda's arm, she peered off through the trees as something bright red fluttered and flapped at them in the distance.

"It looks like . . ." Lucille squinted and leaned farther out over the railing. "Like . . . a cape?"

"Wait—let me see." Miranda climbed onto the hot tub, following the direction of Lucille's gaze. "It *is* a cape!" She burst out laughing. "It's Nick."

"He's standing up on the railing!" Lucille exclaimed. "Flapping his wings—uh . . . his cape! That idiot—he's going to fall if he's not careful!"

"No, he won't." Miranda laughed again. "Guys like Nick never fall. They're invincible."

"Heyyyy!" Nick's voice floated out to them, and the cape waved wildly. "Hey! How about a hike up the mountain this morning?"

"With you?" Miranda shouted back.

"Who else? I'm the only one who knows where things are around here!"

"Get down from there!" Lucille yelled. "Before you break your neck!"

"What?" Nick hollered.

"I said you're going to break your neck!" Lucille screamed.

"Naw! Won't happen! I'm invincible!"

"See?" Miranda laughed. "I told you."

She turned back into the room with Lucille trailing behind.

"Okay, here's the itinerary," Lucille told her. "It's ten o'clock now. You have plenty of time for breakfast by the pool, for soaking up sun, and for getting in some swimming, if you like. At noon, your aromatherapy. Then lunch, and after that, a makeover—for your face and your hair. We figured this first day should be a little lazy. To help you all recover from jet lag. Sound okay to you?"

"Sounds great."

"Good. Tonight there's dinner at the club, and afterward, a special movie screening in Byron's private theater."

"Will Byron be there?"

"Definitely for dinner. That's my only confirmation so far."

"Oh." Miranda tried not to sound disappointed. "I guess he can't be around for everything."

"Not as busy as he is, no. Well, gotta run. Things to do, people to see." Lucille started out the door when a maid appeared in the hallway and handed her a tissue-wrapped parcel.

"Miss Peterson?" The maid smiled.

"No, but I'll give it to her." Lucille nodded. "Thanks very much." As the maid bowed and backed away, Lucille gave the package to Miranda and waited while she opened it.

"Oh, Lucille." Miranda's eyes widened. "Oh, look at this. . . ."

"What?" Lucille demanded. "Come on, the suspense is killing me."

"There must be some mistake," Miranda said in disbelief. She held up a skimpy bikini and a sheer matching jacket, her eyes going wide. "This can't be for me. I can't wear this—I *wouldn't* wear this!"

"Why not, may I ask? You certainly have the figure for it. And if you've got it, flaunt it, that's my motto."

"Lucille—*look* at this!"

"I *am* looking. It's making me jealous as hell. You'll look darling in it, Miranda. Zena's a genius—she can figure your most flattering style and color with just a glance. Oh, don't be so shy. Remember—this is a *fantasy* trip. You can do things here you'd never do at home."

"Only if you swear not to take any pictures and show them to my parents."

"I swear." Lucille laughed and waved, leaving Miranda alone to try on her new swimsuit.

Zena *was* a genius, Miranda had to admit. The style was perfect for her figure, and the tiny blue and lilac pattern brought out the deep blue of her eyes. Miranda got dressed, then stood before the full-length mirror, staring at herself in awe. Was that really her? Why, she looked almost . . .

"Glamorous," said a voice behind her, and Miranda whirled around with a gasp.

"Nick! How long have you been here!"

Nick was posed just inside the French doors, both sides of his cape held out like giant wings. As his eyes swept her appreciatively from head to toe, Miranda blushed and quickly grabbed for the jacket on her bed. Nick just as quickly snatched it out of her reach.

"Come on, Nick! I need that!"

"Trust me, you don't need a thing. Except my arms around you. And don't worry about my entrance—unfortunately for me, you were already decent when I landed."

Miranda gave an exasperated sigh. *"How'd* you get in here?"

Nick swirled the cape around his shoulders. "I flew."

"Hmmm. The trouble is, I almost believe you."

"Believe me. It's true. You going down to the pool?"

"I think that's the plan."

"Kelly and Jo are already there. Jo's attacking the scrambled eggs, and Kelly's attacking the pool man."

Miranda laughed again. "The pool man?"

"Well, he's not fighting her off, that's for sure. You know, I think I might actually have a chance with Kelly—she seems to like anything that's male and breathing."

"Then by all means, why don't you go annoy Kelly?"

"'Cause I like you better. What about our hike?"

"I don't know. I'm not sure I'll have time today."

"Lame, Miranda. Lame, lame, lame. You know as well as I do, your morning's free. I promise to be a perfect gentleman. We'll even bring Jo and Kelly along if you want."

"Well . . ."

"Jo for you, Kelly for me. What do you say?"

"No."

"Could you be a little more definite?"

"Definitely no."

"Come on. Make a date with me, and I'll give you back your little coat here. Not that it'll hide much, by the looks of it."

"Does Peg know you're harassing the guests?"

"Ooh—you play dirty." Nick tossed her the jacket, then leaped onto the balcony. "Have a nice swim! Watch out for sharks!"

"Yeah, and don't fly into any tall buildings," Miranda countered. She put on her jacket and headed downstairs, determined to memorize the route this time so she could find her way back again.

A scrumptious buffet had been arranged on the terrace. Chilled glasses of freshly squeezed juice, eggs fixed three different ways, bacon, ham, sausage, an array of delicious fruits, homemade muffins, yogurt, and cereals. Jo waved eagerly as Miranda came out beside the pool; Kelly bestowed her a regal wave.

"You really scared me last night!" Jo grabbed her in a big hug. "What happened to you?"

"I guess I was more tired than I thought," Miran-

da joked. "But I'm fine now. Ready for anything."
She stepped back and eyed Jo in amusement. "Jo,
why on earth are you out here in your sweats?"

"Oh, big mystery there! Look around you, Miranda. Two teeny little mermaids—and one beached
whale!"

"Oh, stop it! You'd look cute in a swimsuit!"

"I'd look fat. I *am* fat!"

"You are not!"

"Miranda, I see myself in the mirror every day,
and I pride myself on being a realist. I'm *fat*—end of
discussion. Besides, I already told you I burn in the
sun. So while you and Kelly get nice golden tans, I'm
going to enjoy the air-conditioning. *Inside!*"

"Kelly already has a nice golden tan." Miranda
lowered her voice to a whisper. "Why is she sitting
under a tree, do you know?"

"Because she's an alien being, and nothing she
does makes any sense to me."

"Well, do you have to leave? I don't particularly
want to spend my time with Kelly—I'd rather be
with you."

"Well, *I'm* going to play Ping-Pong, if you must
know."

"Are you serious?"

"You should see this game room they have here—
it's fantastic. Robert challenged me to a Ping-Pong
tournament, but he's in for a big surprise if he thinks
he's going to win!"

"You're leaving now?" Miranda threw a longing
glance at the pool, then back at Jo.

"I'm leaving this very second. If you get bored,
just follow the sound of the bouncing balls."

Miranda watched Jo go off. Then she filled her plate and walked over to where Kelly was lounging in the shade.

"Hi, Kelly—how's it going? Don't you want to get some sun?"

Kelly shrugged. "Sun's bad for you."

"But you have such a wonderful tan—"

"I use a salon," Kelly informed her, as though Miranda must truly be the dullest girl in the world. "Don't you know you can get skin cancer from sitting out here?"

"Well, can't tanning booths be just as dangerous?"

Kelly's stare was blank, and Miranda hid a smile.

"How about a quick dip in the pool, then?" Miranda couldn't help adding, "You can stay underwater."

"I don't want to ruin my hair." Kelly yawned. She stood up, swishing her long black hair back and forth over her shoulders. Her legs were long and perfectly shaped, Miranda noticed. Her toenails were painted hot pink.

"I see," Miranda said, not seeing at all.

"This is a stupid pool," Kelly complained. "All these weird statues standing around. God, I feel like they're all watching me."

Don't flatter yourself, Miranda wanted to say, but managed to restrain herself.

"And anyway"—Kelly pouted—"that dog keeps jumping in. I hate dogs."

Miranda looked where she was pointing. A big white sheepdog was paddling in the shallow end of the swimming pool, its thick hair plastered down, its tongue lolling happily.

"Whose dog is it?" Miranda asked.

"How should I know? But he's getting hair in the pool." Kelly made a disgusted face. "I'm going inside. Zena said she'd show me some designs she's been working on for a new wardrobe for Byron."

"Oh. Okay, see you." Miranda sighed and finished her breakfast, throwing tidbits into the pool, which the dog promptly caught in his mouth. When her food was finally gone, she carried her plate back to the table, and the dog climbed out, shaking water all over the furniture. After a few quick sniffs just to make sure Miranda wasn't hiding any more snacks, the dog trotted off into the garden.

Well, Miranda, just you and me now, kid.

The pool looked so lovely, so inviting. Miranda found an inner tube and threw it in, then dived off the board, loving that first icy shock of water against her skin. She swam several laps, then rested awhile at the edge. Nymphs and sprites and goddesses regarded her benignly from all around, but other than that, the terrace was deserted. Someone had left a pair of sunglasses lying on the side, and she grabbed them before swimming off again. Plunging underwater, she resurfaced inside the inner tube and lay back upon it, her head resting on the rim, her hair flowing out in the water, the sun warm and gentle on her face.

Heaven, she thought delightedly. *I've died and gone to heaven.*

The water made little lapping sounds around her head. Lulling sounds. Lulling her into a light, lazy sleep.

Miranda closed her eyes. She bobbed slowly in the

water, kicking her legs from time to time, but mostly just lying there, peacefully floating. It was very still. Just the birds and that soft rippling sound and the hot, sleepy sun . . .

She dozed. So restful . . . so relaxed . . .

From somewhere far away came a muffled splash. *That dog again,* Miranda thought lazily. *He's probably come back to see if I have any food.*

Lifting her head, she peered off across the pool. She saw the dog standing on the steps in the shallow end, holding a ball in his mouth. She called to him, but when he didn't respond, she lounged back and closed her eyes once more.

Little waves ruffled around her. She stretched out one arm and let her fingers trail in the water.

And then, suddenly, she felt a prickling over her skin.

Not the comfortable sort of prickling the sun makes . . . but a different sort of feeling. An *unnerving* sort of sensation . . .

Almost as if . . .

As if I'm being watched.

Miranda frowned and straightened up. She shoved the sunglasses onto her forehead and squinted hard across the water.

The dog was gone.

The pool . . . the terrace . . . the gardens— everything seemed normal and quiet. The only things watching her were the white marble eyes of the statues.

It's me, she thought nervously. *Just me. I haven't had a real vacation for so long, I don't even know how to relax.*

She took a deep breath. She lay back, settled the sunglasses in place, and determinedly shut her eyes.

"Miranda . . ."

This time she bolted upright. This time she *knew* she hadn't imagined it. *Someone* had whispered to her. *Someone* had said her name.

A cold chill snaked through Miranda's body. Cautiously she began paddling toward the edge of the pool, toward the spot where she'd heard the voice.

"Hello?" she called. "Is someone there?"

No one answered. Nothing moved.

And then she realized someone *was* there.

As Miranda swam nearer, she saw a shape—a dark, indistinct shape—lurking just behind one of the statues. She flung off the sunglasses, trying to see, but the sun was so bright now, directly in her eyes, that everything began to blur.

"Who's there!" she called again.

Slowly the shape pulled back and disappeared. Miranda stopped in alarm.

"Who *are* you! What do you want?"

There was no warning.

Just a slight tremor as the statue began to tip.

And then the crash . . .

The swift downward plunge as she felt herself being pushed to the very bottom of the pool . . .

The water rushing full force into her lungs.

13

Miranda thrashed wildly.

In some vague realm of consciousness she knew she was upside down, knew that her legs were trapped in the deflated coils of her inner tube. Gasping desperately, she finally managed to kick herself free and struggle to the surface.

She broke through at last, coughing and choking. For several minutes she treaded water, gulping deep breaths of air, and then she made for the shallow end.

She huddled there alone on the steps, her eyes scanning the terrace, the lawns, the gardens. On the opposite side of the pool she could see the empty spot where the statue had been, but no one was there now.

Only shadows . . . only . . .

Miranda frowned. Shadows? There *were* shadows there, she could see them clearly, but they were *different* shadows, not the one she'd seen before, not the one that had seemed so human. . . .

But it was *human, I* know *it was.* Someone *was there.*

She was shaking all over, in spite of the blazing sun, in spite of the hot, dry breeze.

It could have fallen right on top of me. . . . It could have crushed me . . . knocked me completely out. . . . I could have drowned.

Tears stung her eyes. She could have died so easily, and no one would have seen or heard. No one would even have known.

I heard my name.

The thought struck her, cold and hard. In her terrible panic she'd forgotten about it until just this second. That's why she'd swum to that side in the first place. Because someone had whispered her name. *"Miranda . . ."*

But now the whole idea seemed crazy. Impossible! Who would have done such a horrible thing? And why?

Miranda got out of the pool. She walked shakily around to the opposite side, and then she stopped, gazing down at the stones of the terrace.

Water had splashed everywhere.

She wasn't exactly sure what she'd expected to find, but if there *had* been any sort of evidence, it'd been completely washed away.

She stared down into the depths of the pool. The statue lay on the bottom, looking up at her with blank, white eyes.

Miranda hurried into the house. She wanted to tell someone what had happened, but there didn't seem to be anyone around. She wished she could find Jo or Lucille or even Kelly, but she didn't have the faintest idea where to look for them. After several wrong turns, she finally found the way upstairs to her room and locked the door behind her.

"You know how it is when you feel someone watching you—when you feel eyes staring at the back of your head?"

Byron's words echoed through her mind, and she fought to block them out. Maybe she *was* getting a little paranoid, she had to admit—talking with Byron yesterday had certainly given her something to think about.

Frowning, she leaned her head upon the door and closed her eyes. She'd tried not to dwell on it this morning, tried not to puzzle over it after she'd gone to bed last night. But how could she *not* be concerned? Byron might be overworked and stressed out, but there was no disputing the fact that he was also frightened, and everyone seemed to be ignoring that.

She drew a deep breath. She was still trembling, and she willed herself to be calm. Once again the scrawled message in the autograph book flashed through her mind—IF I CAN'T HAVE YOU, NO ONE CAN. She wished she knew where Byron was right now. She wished she could find him and tell him what had just happened to her.

Miranda opened her eyes. She pressed both hands to her temples and rubbed them gently.

I've got to stop thinking like this. Even if Byron's

suspicions are true, what would I have to do with it? I'm sure there's a perfectly logical explanation. Be-sides, Nick said the house was really old, didn't he? Those statues are probably ancient, too. I just hap-pened to be in the wrong place at the wrong time.

She wanted so much to convince herself that nothing was wrong. She went into the bathroom, wrapped herself in an oversize bathtowel, then sat down on the edge of the bed. She had to gather her thoughts together—had to think.

She couldn't sit still. She got up and walked to the balcony, leaning over the railing and into the sun-shine. Peering off toward the garage, she found herself thinking of Nick, halfway expecting him to appear. She wished she could spot that silly red cape. She needed something to make her laugh right now. She needed someone to talk to.

She also needed some clothes.

Miranda went back in and opened the closet where she'd hung her things last night. To her dismay, the closet was empty. *Oh, great, now what am I going to do?* She couldn't run around in this skimpy little thing till her suitcase showed up—and what had happened to those clothes Zena had prom-ised her in the meantime?

She jumped as the telephone rang by her bed. Who on earth would be calling her here? Cautiously she lifted the receiver, surprised to hear a familiar voice.

"Miranda—it's Byron."

"Byron?" Instantly the swimming pool flashed through her mind—the statue falling—the voice calling—

"Miranda?" Byron was speaking again. "Hey, are you there?"

"Yes . . . yes . . . I'm here."

"How'd you like to go for a drive?"

"Now?"

"Of course now."

"You mean the three of us? Kelly and Jo and—"

"No, just you." She could hear a smile in his voice. "But don't tell anyone—I'm not even supposed to be here this morning."

"Byron, I can't go off and leave the others. It wouldn't be right!"

"Kelly and Jo have plenty to occupy their time."

"And I'm supposed to get a massage!"

"Miranda, believe me. I can handle a massage, if that's all you're worried about."

Miranda chuckled in spite of herself. "That's not what I meant. It's just that they've planned all these things for us, and I feel like I should be here."

"Feel spontaneous instead. Think you can find the pool?"

"Byron, about the pool—"

"Go out to the swimming pool. If you walk along the north side for about twenty yards, the path will cut straight into some trees. Just through there, you'll see a gazebo. Go behind that, and there'll be a gate in the brick wall."

"I'm with you so far."

"Great. I'll be waiting for you on the other side."

"What if somebody sees me?"

"Nobody will see you. Most of the staff is off today, and the rest of them are in a big meeting with Peg."

"Byron, there's one more little thing."

"What's that?"

"I don't have any clothes."

"No clothes? I promise I won't let that bother me."

"I'm really serious. My suitcase still hasn't gotten here, and all I've got are these swim things. I can't go anywhere without clothes."

"I'll take care of the problem." Byron was smiling again. "See you in a minute."

Miranda hung up, then stood there staring down at the telephone. *Byron Slater just called and asked me to go for a drive with him. Alone. Oh, my God, this can't be happening to me.*

As quickly as she could, she slipped through the house and out to the terrace. Byron was right—there still didn't seem to be anyone around, and she had no trouble locating the path or the gazebo. She went out the gate and immediately found herself in a narrow alleyway, deserted except for one shiny red Porsche convertible and its occupant.

Byron yelled her name and leaned out over the side.

"Hey, lady, want a ride?"

"You must be extremely desperate for passengers," Miranda retorted teasingly.

"Oh, come on. Isn't it okay that I just want to be with you?"

"You're crazy, Byron."

"Well, I have to admit, that's not the *first* time I've ever been told that."

Miranda couldn't help but laugh. She climbed into the passenger side, and Byron sped away. For one wild minute she actually thought they might crash through the gates at the end of the drive, but just as she drew in her breath, the gates opened and the car zoomed through.

Once on the road Byron reached behind him and pulled a bundle of clothes from the floor. He tossed it to her, and Miranda gave it a quick appraisal.

"For me?"

"Well, actually they're some of *my* clothes!" Byron raised his voice, trying to speak over the roar of the engine. "They'll be a little big on you, but if anyone sees us, maybe they'll think you're my brother!"

"Hey, I don't know if I like that or not!"

Byron gave her his famous smile and floored the accelerator. "Hang on!"

Miranda tried not to watch the road careening away beneath their tires. She slipped into an oversize T-shirt and tucked her hair up under a baseball cap, then wriggled into a pair of gym shorts and pulled the drawstring tight around her waist. Byron flashed her an admiring look.

"I never looked *that* good in those clothes!"

"No? What about your brother?"

"I don't have a brother!" Byron laughed and reached over to tug the brim of her cap.

They rode on and on. The mountains were getting steeper now, Miranda noticed—the terrain a lot more rugged. From time to time she caught a glimpse of the valley below, growing farther and farther away.

"You like camping?" Byron shouted.

"Don't know! Never been!"

"Maybe it's time you found out!"

"Meaning?"

"Meaning maybe we could all come up and camp while you're here! You and your two friends!"

"Somehow I don't see Kelly being very excited about that!"

Byron made a face. "Somehow I don't see Kelly being very excited about anything!"

They kept driving. After several more miles of winding curves, Byron suddenly turned the car off onto another road—an unpaved, narrower road—which seemed to Miranda to lead almost straight up the side of the mountain.

"Where are we going?" she asked him.

"You'll see!"

He was driving more slowly now, the car bouncing over rocks and deep ruts. The landscape here was even more thickly wooded, with a certain rough wildness to it. As though this part of the world had never been inhabited . . . never been tamed. And as the car came out at last at the top, coming to a stop in the midst of a wide spacious clearing, Miranda caught her breath at the absolute beauty of it. From here she could see the whole valley spreading out below them. As though there were two separate and distinct worlds—the one beneath, and the one here above, alone, with Byron.

"Peaceful, isn't it."

Byron's words startled her. She realized suddenly that the silence, too, was unlike anything she'd ever experienced before. Calm and still and untouched by the noise of civilization.

"It's so wonderful," she murmured, and Byron broke into a smile.

"Come on," he said. He got out and came around to open her door. "I want to show you something."

She hadn't even noticed the cabin at first. So camouflaged was it, nestled back beneath huge old trees, that she had to look twice to see it. And then she realized it wasn't actually complete at all, but more of a shell, still in the process of being built. She could see the sturdy logs of its walls, the roofline and tall rock chimney, but all around it lay piles of lumber and abandoned tools.

"It's my house," Byron said quietly.

"You mean, your summer house?" Miranda asked, but Byron shook his head.

"No. My *real* house."

"But I thought—"

"That's Peg's house." Byron sighed. "And Robert's house, and Zena's and all the others'. That house down there is Byron-Slater-the-Star's house." His voice lowered, and he shook his head. "But it's not mine."

Miranda reached out and touched his arm. "Are you building this yourself?"

"Yes. Nick's been helping me, but the original idea was mine. The design, the plans, everything. We've done it all, just the two of us. It's going to be so great when it's finished. Just a place where I can come and get away from everyone and everything." He glanced at her, his voice almost shy. "Would you like to see it?"

"I'd love to see it."

"I was hoping you'd say that."

He took her hand and led her across the clearing. Together they went up the front steps onto the wide porch, and Byron pushed open the door, steering her inside.

"There's still so much to be done," he informed her, pointing out things as he led her through. Miranda gazed at the lofty beamed ceiling, the massive stone fireplace, the open spaces for windows. The whole place smelled of cedar and sawdust, of pine trees and clean fresh air.

After the tour they went out on the back porch, and again Miranda had to catch her breath in amazement. The view here was even better than the view in front. She felt as if she were standing at the very top of the universe.

"It's best at night," Byron broke into her thoughts. "You feel as if you can just reach right out and touch the stars, they're so close."

"Do you ever sleep here?"

"Only on rare occasions. When I can manage to sneak away." He winked at her. "Sometimes Nick and I bring sleeping bags and camp out. I own all this land around here, so nobody bothers us." He paused a minute, his voice going almost wistful. "I feel safe here, Miranda."

She turned and stared at him. She could feel her heart aching inside, and suddenly, more than anything, she wished she could protect Byron from all the awful things troubling him.

They sat on the porch, and they talked. They talked about everything in the world, it seemed to

Miranda, and they talked for so long, she lost all track of time. She could actually see Byron loosening up. She could see the change in him as he began to relax and smile more often, as his laugh came more readily, as his conversation grew more candid. Stories about his past, his family, school days, old friends left behind. Hopes for the future, his journey to fame and fortune. Incidents that had taken place during the making of his movies—some of them serious, some dangerous, others funny. He talked about the expectations that had been thrust upon him, the destructive ways he'd dealt with them in the past, the pride he felt now for having straightened himself out. He spoke of the demands he was now forced to meet—demands from his public, his fans, his press, his mentors, his staff—and, most of all, himself.

"I'm not alone in this, Miranda," he kept reminding her over and over again. "I'm not the only star who's ever had to go through all this stuff. Some of them make it, and some of them don't. And I'm determined to have a *life*—I'm determined to have *me.*"

Miranda shook her head in awe. "It sounds so complicated, though. You're like a prisoner. I could never do what you do."

"You have to keep your head on straight. You've got to keep your priorities in line, get a clear perspective." He stared off into the trees, a sad smile playing at the corners of his mouth. "The minute you start believing what your press says about you, you might as well call it quits."

"So you really don't believe it?" Miranda couldn't help teasing. "Big brave macho hero? Casanova? Heartbreaker? And what did I just read in that one magazine last month . . . sexiest man alive?"

She thought he might actually have blushed a little. "How could any girl ever have the patience to know me? You have to be so many different things to so many different people in this business. There are all those layers to peel through."

"Well, I know some girls who really enjoy peeling off layers," Miranda teased again.

Byron glanced down at her, amused. "Is that a proposition, Miss Peterson?"

"No. And don't start using your movie lines on me."

He laughed and slipped an arm around her shoulder. "It'd take someone really special to put up with this kind of life. People watching you all the time, putting words in your mouth. All the pettiness and jealousy and phoniness. It's no wonder celebrities have so much trouble maintaining any kind of normal relationship with anybody."

"But you *have* had relationships—and some pretty serious ones, from what I've read."

"Hmmm. This sounds like it's turning into an interview."

Miranda laughed. "See? I'm no different from any other fan. I believe at least *half* of everything I read about you."

"And I thought you were different," Byron teased back. He lowered his head, looking a little embarrassed. "Actually, most of them were just good friends."

"Oh, right. Now I've heard everything."

"Really!" He laughed, giving her shoulders a squeeze. "Don't you know the media always blows everything out of proportion!"

"Uh-huh . . ."

"Anyway, I'm not *encouraged* to have relationships with anyone," he added, his tone going dry.

Miranda shot him a curious look. "Why not?"

"Can't you guess? It might affect my popularity. I might not be such a heartthrob if girls think I'm already taken." He shook his head with an ironic smile. "Being obtainable is part of my Great Image. Part of the Great Fantasy. Or so I'm told."

Again Miranda felt a tug at her heart. "By who?" she demanded.

"Peg." Byron hesitated, then gave a humorless laugh. "But then she's always supposed to know what's best for my career, isn't she?"

Miranda didn't answer. She hadn't found Peg very likable so far, and she couldn't imagine Byron ever having had a relationship with the woman. Considering his remark, she tilted her head back so that she could gaze up into the cloudless blue sky.

"I can't even imagine your world," she said softly. "Not in a million years. It's so alien to me."

His arm tightened around her. Gently he pulled her closer, so that her head rested against his shoulder.

"It *is* an alien world. And everyone thinks it's such a wonderful world, but to tell you the truth, some of it—a *lot* of it—isn't a very nice place at all."

Miranda turned back to him. "I'm sorry, Byron. I really am."

His dark eyes held her. He lifted one hand and gently brushed a strand of hair back from her forehead.

"Do you have a boyfriend back home?" he asked her.

The question caught Miranda off guard. "Me?"

Byron pretended to look around. "Is there someone else here I should be asking?"

"No." Miranda laughed. "No boyfriend."

"Why is that? Too particular?"

Sure, Byron, I've got an army of guys beating down my door. "It pays to be particular," she replied.

"I couldn't agree more. That's why I asked *you* to come with me today."

Miranda shoved him in the side with her elbow. "Don't be a jerk. I'll have a week here, and then I'll fly home, and then I'll never see you again. You'll go on being a famous star, and I'll go on being a nobody who starts college in the fall. I don't want any misunderstandings between us, Byron. No lies or promises or heartbreaks, either. I just want my life to be nice and normal. And happy, too, if at all possible."

"Whoa!" Byron pulled away, his eyes widening in mock alarm. "All I said was—"

"I know what you said, and it sounds very well rehearsed."

He chuckled. "You're not real trusting, are you?"

"No."

"Not even with me?"

"Especially not with you," she threw back at him. They looked at each other, then burst out laughing.

"Touché." Byron nodded, giving her a hug. "I think you could turn out to be dangerous."

At the mention of the word, Miranda's smile faded. She put a hand on Byron's knee and patted him gently.

"Byron," she said, frowning, "something weird happened this morning. It's probably nothing—it's just that after our talk last night . . ."

Her voice trailed off. Byron redirected his gaze onto her face and said softly, "Go on."

"I'm probably overreacting." Miranda's frown deepened. "In fact, now that I think about it—"

"Now that you're thinking about it," Byron prompted her, "you *probably* should tell me."

"Well . . . there was an accident at the pool."

Byron raised an eyebrow. "You mean Caesar? Oh, no, I'm sorry about that. I've told Paul a million times to keep that stupid dog out of the pool—but this is the first time I've ever heard about him—"

"No, not *that* kind of accident!" Miranda shook her head impatiently. "It was one of the statues. It . . . sort of . . . fell on me."

"What!"

"Well, actually, it fell on my inner tube—but it knocked me under, and I almost didn't get up again."

Quickly Miranda related her near-fiasco, the strange voice she thought she'd heard, the eerie feeling she'd had of being watched. As she talked, she could feel Byron's grip tightening around her shoulders, his body going tense.

"Nick told me the house is old," she finished

hurriedly, "so I don't want to jump to conclusions. In fact, I feel kind of stupid about it now. The whole thing seems pretty unreal."

Byron said nothing. After a while she looked up to see him staring off into the distance, a hard line of worry between his brows.

"I know those statues aren't in great shape," he admitted reluctantly. "Robert said one of the architects talked to him about it just last week." He hesitated, his voice lowering. "I didn't know it was that bad, though. God, Miranda, you could have been . . ."

His eyes shifted onto hers. His face looked strained and . . . *what?* Miranda thought. *Frightened?*

"It's okay," Miranda assured him hastily. "I just thought you should know, is all. Before someone really *does* get hurt."

Again Byron kept silent. He looked down at the ground, and very slowly his arm slid from around her shoulders.

"Maybe . . ." he said at last, his voice barely above a whisper. "Maybe you should stay away from me."

She turned toward him in surprise. "Why?"

"I mean . . . maybe *I'm* the reason you're in danger."

"What do you mean?" she protested, though her heart chilled within her. "Are you saying you *don't* think it was just an accident? That someone *deliberately* tried to hurt me?"

"Well, it makes sense, doesn't it?" His smile was grim as he ran both hands back through his hair.

"With those phone calls and the message in that book? And now, if they know how much I like you . . ."

"Byron, stop." Miranda gave a nervous laugh. "I only met you yesterday. They couldn't possibly know something you don't even know yourself—"

"If they know how much I like you," he went on as though she hadn't spoken, "then getting to you is just another way—a *closer* way—of getting to me."

Despite the warmth of the sun, Miranda felt chilled. She stared at his profile without speaking, then jumped as Byron got abruptly to his feet.

"Damn," he muttered. "I'm late for another interview. And you're late for lunch. Peg won't be happy with either one of us."

"What are you going to tell her?"

"I'll think of something." He paused, then offered a faint smile. "I always do."

He reached out and helped Miranda to her feet. Together they walked back to the car, but before Miranda could climb inside, Byron pulled her gently toward him, pressing her lightly against his chest. For an endless moment he gazed down at her without speaking. She could feel the quickening of his heartbeat; she could see the strange dark lights in his eyes.

"Thank you, Miranda," he murmured.

She drew back from him a little, fixing him with a quizzical smile. "For what?"

"For being here. For letting me share this place with you."

Miranda didn't know what to say. She felt his fingertips slide beneath the tip of her chin, tilting her head back. And then his kiss, long and deep, before he finally released her and helped her into the car.

They drove several miles without speaking. Byron seemed completely lost in thought now, both his hands on the steering wheel, his face set in a frown. Miranda stared out her window, but her mind wasn't on the scenery—it was on Byron and the kiss still lingering warm upon her lips.

The road seemed steeper than it had before. As Miranda continued to watch from her window, it slowly began to dawn on her how high they'd actually climbed. Heading back now in the opposite direction, she had an unobstructed view of their descent, the narrowness of the road, the sharpness of the curves. Without even thinking she reached out for Byron and lay her hand on his knee. She felt his thigh muscles clench as he applied pressure to the brake and shifted into low gear.

"Does it always look this scary going down?" Miranda tried to laugh, but her voice trembled instead.

Byron's eyes remained on the road. His fingers tightened upon the wheel.

"Don't worry," he assured her. "I know this road so well, I could drive it in my sleep."

As if to prove his point, he expertly maneuvered a hairpin turn, while Miranda sucked in her breath.

"See?" He smiled at her. "Nothing to it."

Miranda started breathing again and managed a weak nod. "Great, Byron. I believe you."

"You *are* with a superhero, you know."

"Uh-huh. Just keep reminding me."

He glanced over at her with a smile.

And then the car gave a violent lurch.

Miranda saw the wheel spinning in Byron's hands—his instant look of surprise.

And then another jolt—another lurch—

"What is it?" she cried. "What's wrong?"

But the car was swerving now, back and forth, sliding from one side of the road to the other—the mountain to their right—the valley to their left.

Miranda sat frozen in horror.

She heard the squeal of the tires, she felt the car shuddering around her.

And then she saw the guardrail.

Just a thin band of metal stretching between them and eternity . . .

"Oh, my God," she whispered. "We're going over."

14

Miranda felt the impact—heard the scrape and slivering and crush of metal as the car sideswiped the railing and kept on sliding. It went into a spin, and then suddenly—miraculously—they were stopped.

Silence crashed down around them.

Silence so deep, so thick, that Miranda thought for one second that she actually might have died.

She looked down and saw that she was still strapped into her seat.

She looked over and saw Byron sitting stunned beside her.

And then she turned and looked out her window, and a hoarse cry caught in her throat.

The passenger side of the car—*her* side—was tipped off the embankment, just past the end of the

132

guardrail, hanging there inches above the sheer drop of the precipice.

"Byron," she whispered.

"Miranda, are you okay?"

"Byron . . . look."

She was afraid to move. She felt him shifting beside her, and as she summoned the courage to look back at him, she could see how pale he was. His eyes narrowed, as though he were making a swift assessment of their predicament, and then his hand came down reassuringly on her shoulder.

"Don't worry, Miranda. I'm going to get you out of here, and you're going to be just fine."

Somehow she managed a nod. Her eyes blurred with frightened tears, and she bravely forced them away.

"Miranda," she heard his voice, and she saw his famous, familiar smile, trying to encourage her, trying to soothe her, "you trust me, don't you."

It was a statement, not a question, and she carefully nodded her head. "Yes."

"Good girl. Now—very slowly—lean this way. Slowly—no sudden moves. Just start leaning toward me, and no matter what happens, or what you hear, just keep leaning, just keep reaching out for me. Got it?"

Miranda gulped and nodded again.

"Okay, here we go."

Through a haze of sheer terror she heard the sound of his door opening. Through the haze of sheer panic she felt the car rock ever so slightly.

"You're doing fine—you're doing great," Byron

assured her. She could see his body, silhouetted there in the door of the car, and *he's getting out,* her mind raced, *he's leaving without me and the car's going to fall—how did he get out so fast, I didn't even see him move and now he's out there where it's safe, he's out there looking in at me and he's smiling and I'm too afraid to move or even breathe. . . .*

From some faraway place she heard a groan. From some faraway place she felt the car shift beneath her.

Her fingers fumbled at the seatbelt. She closed her eyes and swallowed down a sick taste of fear. She opened them again and focused on Byron's face.

"Don't stop, Miranda," his voice said calmly. "Just keep moving toward me."

"I'm scared—"

"Keep moving. That's fine."

"I'm *scared* to move—"

"Just keep coming. Don't be afraid."

The whole thing seemed like a dream. Byron's face in the open doorway, Byron's arms stretched out. And like a dream she felt Byron's arms close around her at last, pulling her to safety, holding her close.

"It's okay, Miranda," he mumbled in her ear. "I've got you. You're fine now."

For endless moments she couldn't speak. When at last she was able to raise her head and look around, she stared at the car perched precariously on the edge of the road.

"What happened?" she mumbled. "Did a tire blow out?"

His answer was grim. "I don't know. Stay here. I'm going to check this out."

Miranda sat down on the ground. She sat down hard and pulled her legs up to her chest and rested her chin on top of her knees. She saw Byron examine the sides and back of the car; she saw the hood lift up and Byron disappear beneath it.

"Be careful!" she shouted.

But no sooner had the words left her mouth than she heard a chilling sound which made her jump to her feet in terror.

"Byron!" she screamed. "Watch out!"

For one split second the car teetered on the ledge—the next second it had simply vanished over the cliff. As Miranda watched horrified, she saw Byron jump clear and land several yards away. Then, from far below, came the fiery blast of an explosion.

"Oh, my God!" She ran to him, helping him up, brushing him off. "Are you okay? Are you hurt? Oh, my God, you could have been killed!"

"I'm okay," he assured her breathlessly.

"But your car! Your car's gone!"

"Jesus, Miranda, I can get another car." He took a swipe at one cheek smearing the blood there, then immediately spun around. Shading his eyes from the sun, he scanned the cliffs above them, the mounds of rock, the brush and trees and scrubby patches of undergrowth.

"What?" Miranda demanded. "What is it?"

A bird screeched loudly, circling in the sky. Other than that, there was no sound . . . no movement.

"We need to get out of here," Byron mumbled. "We need to go right now."

"You're really scaring me," Miranda said. "What's going on?"

"Nothing," Byron said, forcing her around, giving her a push. "Hurry up. Go!"

"Not till you tell me what's wrong," Miranda insisted. "You found something, didn't you? Did someone do something to the car? Is that what you're not telling me?"

"Just go, Miranda."

"But how could anyone have done that? Nobody knows where we are!"

"Someone could have followed us up here— waited for us to leave it. There was plenty of time to do something to the car while we were at the cabin."

"So what you're saying," Miranda kept babbling, even as Byron kept pushing her, "is that this *wasn't* an accident. That somebody did this on purpose. That somebody wanted us . . ."

She couldn't say the word. She couldn't even think it.

"Dead," Byron finished for her. "And now I don't have a shred of evidence, so no one's going to believe me about this, either. Come on, I want to get off this road."

"You think whoever did this is still out here, don't you? You think they're still going to come after us!"

"I don't know what to think," Byron muttered. "Except that I should never have brought you up here with me."

Clambering up the side of the mountain, Byron pulled her up after him. Miranda gritted her teeth and tried to keep her balance, but rocks and holes made the going rough. She felt one foot slide out from under her, and as she cried out and started to slip, she also heard Byron give a loud yell.

"Hey!" he shouted. "Up here!"

Stunned, Miranda felt him steady her, and the next thing she knew, Byron was sliding back down toward the road. She could see a Land Rover stopped in the narrow lane, and Nick waving wildly from the widow.

"Hi, you two!" He grinned. "Going my way?"

15

Am I glad to see you!" Byron greeted him.

"Well, you're not going to be glad to see Peg," Nick warned. "She's about ready to have a cow. What the hell are you doing? Mountain climbing?"

"You could say that. Come on, get us out of here." Byron flung open the door and pushed Miranda inside. Nick threw her a puzzled glance in the rearview mirror.

"And who's this?" He pretended to study Miranda. "Your brother?"

Miranda gave him a withering glare, and Nick pulled back in mock fear.

"Whoa! Just kidding!"

"Go, Nick." As Byron slid into the front, Nick obligingly gunned the engine and took off. After several miles, he finally found a spot wide enough to turn around in, then headed back toward home.

For a long time they rode in silence. Miranda could see only part of Nick's face in the mirror, his eyes darting toward Byron from time to time. Byron sat stiffly beside him, gazing out the window.

"So what gives, my man?" Nick ventured at last. "Where's your car?"

Byron nodded toward the sheer drop at the opposite side of the road. "Somewhere down there."

"What!"

"The car went out on me, Nick," Byron said quietly. "It's a miracle we weren't killed."

"Come on, Byron, you know I always check out the cars before you drive them. And I went over that baby first thing this morning, hood to tailpipe."

For a long moment Byron didn't answer. He stretched his arm out the open window, his fingers spread wide to the wind.

"Well, then, someone must have followed us up to the cabin," he murmured. "Someone must have . . ." His voice trailed away.

Nick frowned and leaned forward over the wheel. "Jesus, Byron, what are you saying?"

"You know what I'm saying."

"Did you *see* anybody following you?"

Byron shook his head.

"And why didn't you bring Harley with you, anyway? Or me? It's a stupid thing to do, going out alone—especially under the circumstances—especially with—"

Abruptly Nick broke off. He glanced again at Byron, who sighed and turned to face him.

"I've told Miranda about it, Nick. For whatever it's worth."

"God, Byron." Nick bounced back against the seat and swatted his hair from his forehead. "Why'd you do that? What are you trying to do, scare her to death?"

"Well, we sort of have a bond now, don't you think?" Byron returned acidly. "I mean, we *were* almost killed together. I think that brings two people closer, don't you?"

"Byron—"

"Someone tampered with the car, Nick. It worked fine when we left the house, and then it went off the road. But since no one's ever going to be able to *examine* it now, I think it's safe to assume I'm just having delusions again."

"Hey, man, nobody thinks that."

"You know they do." Byron stared at him, his voice lowering. "I'm in trouble here, Nick. Why won't you help me out?"

"Look, Byron, you've got a house full of people. If you start talking about this, there'll be a panic and rumors and all kinds of bad press—not to mention Peg's bad temper! You can't afford any of that right now."

"You mean, in my fragile state?"

"I didn't mean that! All I meant was—"

"Never mind. Just get us home."

Byron lapsed into silence. Nick shot Miranda a helpless look, then fixed his eyes on the road. The trip seemed shorter going back. And when the three of them walked into the house, Peg was there waiting.

"I'm sure I don't need to remind you, Byron," Peg said with an icy smile, "that there are two other guests you're supposed to be spending time with. That *all* of them deserve *equal* attention, and that this really isn't a good idea, your running off like this on some little whim—"

"Not now, Peg," Byron said just as coldly. "I'm not in the mood."

He took the stairs two at a time, leaving the others in awkward silence.

"Where'd you find them?" Peg asked Nick.

"They . . ." Nick took a deep breath. "They had an accident."

"Wonderful. I'm sure it'll be all over the tabloids in the morning—"

Nick stared at her, his expression turning grim. "Don't you even want to find out if Miranda's hurt? She could sue, you know."

As if this thought had never occurred to her, Peg whirled to face Miranda. "Forgive me," she apologized, her tone softening as much as Peg's could. "I was just so worried about you—and then so relieved when you showed up—"

"Don't worry," Miranda cut her off with a forced smile. "I won't sue."

"Well." Peg regarded her for a long moment, then turned her attention back to Nick. "You'll take care of anything that needs to be taken care of?"

"I don't think there's anything *left* to be taken care of," Nick replied evasively.

"But if there is," Peg insisted, "you *will* handle it?"

Nick hesitated. He glanced at Miranda, then gave a curt nod. "I'll handle it."

"Fine. Then we're all set, aren't we?" Peg sounded relieved. "Miranda, I'm afraid when you were so late for lunch that we finished without you. But I'm sure I can have a tray sent up to your room."

"I'm not very hungry," Miranda told her. "But I *would* like some clothes, if you can manage that."

An angry line creased Peg's brow. "Still no suitcase? For heaven's sake, Nick, this should be your responsibility—I can't handle every single detail around here. Doesn't anyone know what happened to her luggage?"

Nick shrugged. "Don't yell at me. I'm just the lowly driver."

"Well, go find someone to take care of it."

"You got it. I'll fax Mr. Airplane and get back with you."

Nick clicked his heels and saluted, and as Peg looked on with a scowl, he exited quickly by the front door.

"And you missed your aromatherapy," Peg reminded Miranda, as though this might possibly mean the end of the world.

Miranda nodded. "Sorry. I think I'll go upstairs now."

"Miranda?"

Miranda stopped, one hand gripping the banister of the curved staircase. "Yes?"

"I know I don't have to remind you how very busy Byron is. He has many important obligations, and he can't afford to be . . . distracted. That's why I have everything scheduled so carefully, you understand. When Byron fails to carry out his responsibilities, it reflects badly on all of us. And it could certainly have a negative impact on his career."

Miranda bit her lip, holding back a sharp retort. Instead she managed to say, "Well, I wouldn't want to interfere with that."

"Good." There was a chilly smile in Peg's voice. "I'm glad we understand each other. I'll have Zena send you something to wear. And this afternoon you'll be getting a makeover, so that should help you feel better."

Miranda marched angrily up to her room. That insufferable woman—the nerve of her! She wondered if it ever occurred to Peg—if, indeed, it ever occurred to *anyone* in this house—that Byron had a life, with feelings and thoughts of his own!

She closed her door, then lay back on the bed, trying to absorb everything that had happened. None of it seemed real to her now—it was all too incredible. The swimming pool—the statue— the cabin on the mountain—the car going off the road . . .

Byron's kiss . . .

Miranda frowned and turned over on her stomach, cradling her head on folded arms. Too much was happening way too fast. Good things and bad things—sweet things and horrifying things. She closed her eyes and saw herself hurtling toward the edge of the cliff—remembered the strange, almost distant feeling of realizing she was going to die. And then Byron saving her. And then Nick showing up.

Nick . . .

How lucky for them that Nick had happened along when he did. Maybe she and Byron would still be out there now if it wasn't for Nick. Still out there, trying to escape from some crazy killer . . .

Starstruck?

Miranda moaned softly. It *must* be true, then, that some deranged person was stalking Byron. That this obsessed fan knew where he was and what he was doing. And even worse—as Byron had suggested— that whoever was close to him might be in just as much danger as he was. . . .

Someone knocked on the door.

Miranda bolted up, heart pounding. She glanced uneasily around the room, then called, "Who is it?"

"Zena, my darling. May I come in?"

A brief memory of chiffon and feathers registered in Miranda's brain. She got up and opened the door, jumping back as a tiny figure swept through in a cloud of thick perfume.

"Poor dear of mine," Zena gushed, tossing an armload of clothes upon the bed. "Not to worry, my precious! Zena has come to your rescue!"

Miranda stood there, open-mouthed. Zena was in her usual regalia of long billowy fabric, only this time her turban was of gold lamé, and her feathers hung from earrings, all the way to her shoulders.

"Come, my love." Zena motioned her over and started pointing out ensembles, one by one. "Choose your favorites, my darling. Choose them all, if you like!"

"I . . ." Miranda finally managed to close her mouth. As she watched Zena's dramatic gestures, she could feel her anger and worry starting to melt away. "I only need a few things, actually—"

"Nonsense!" Zena exclaimed. "There is no such thing as 'only a few' in the world of fashion, my dear one! A woman can *never* have too many clothes!" She took Miranda's arm and pulled her the rest of the way. "Stand here. We'll have you irresistible in no time at all, yes?"

"Well . . . thank you. This is really nice of you."

"Take this one—and this one—and this slinky little top here—and these *adorable* shorts, as well! Yes, they are all *you*, my divine one! Byron will be so pleased! You will enchant him even more!"

Miranda gave a nervous laugh. "I don't want to enchant Byron, I—"

"But you do this without trying!" Zena interrupted cheerfully. "Zena knows these things! Yes, my lovely, you enchant our Byron without even trying!" She held up several pairs of long pants and nodded her head, earrings swinging wildly. "But, my poor precious, beware of Peg. She does not like to share Byron, and this is the truth!"

Miranda watched as Zena produced a silk blouse and skirt for her approval. She nodded mechanically, but her thoughts weren't on the clothes.

"I guess Peg and Byron go back a long way," she mentioned casually, and Zena threw her a knowing look.

"This is no secret, *ma chère*. They were close before—and now, it might be said of them that they are even closer."

"You mean, Byron's in love with her?"

"In love with Peg? No, no, no! What I'm meaning

is this—Peg is the only one who stands between our Byron and his public. For a celebrity, you cannot get much closer than this."

"I . . . see."

"Do not worry, my pretty. Byron has admiring eyes for you, without a doubt! And in these clothes—" She pressed her lips together and made little kissing sounds. "In these clothes, my dearest girl, you will have him completely in your power!"

She stood back then, lifting up a long white sundress and a lacy white fringed shawl.

She beamed. "You like, yes?"

"Zena, really, they're all so beautiful. And I've never seen anything like them in the stores—"

"Nor will you ever, my angel. These are Zena *originals!* Yes, yes, I know how you young girls all love your famous and fancy designers, but think of this. *They* will not be around forever, and Zena *will!* And no one else on earth will have these wonderful clothes—only Miranda Peterson!"

"You really did all these yourself?"

"Naturellement. Why do you think our dear Byron *consistently* appears on everyone's best dressed lists?" She broke into a delighted laugh. "Only because of Zena!"

Miranda managed a smile, and Zena tossed the items dramatically back onto the bed.

"And so!" Zena clapped her hands. "It is a success, is it not? I shall see you later, darling one. And no more worries about your missing luggage!"

In a whirl of skirts and feathers, Zena made her exit. Miranda stood staring a moment at the door, then carefully moved the heap of clothing to one side and eased down onto the edge of the bed. Her thoughts were whirling, her mind in a state of confusion. Zena had made it all too clear that Byron was attracted to her—and Peg's insinuations downstairs had told Miranda the same thing. *But look who Byron is, and look who I am. And at the end of the week I'll wake up from this wonderful dream, and it'll all be over. And* I'm *the one who'll have the broken heart . . . and Byron's the one who'll move on to some other romance. . . .*

Get a grip, Miranda, she told herself firmly. Hadn't it been Byron himself who'd talked about keeping one's priorities in line, who'd warned about getting a clear perspective? *So quit being stupid, Miranda Peterson, because you're the one who's going to end up hurt, and you won't have anyone to blame but yourself.*

Looking up, she caught a glimpse of herself in the full-length mirror. Her hair was a mess, and her face looked tired and pale, and as she continued to stare at her reflection, the awful reality of what had happened that morning came back to haunt her.

What were the odds of two near-tragedies happening on the same day? And what were the odds of them nearly happening to her?

Miranda ran one listless hand over the sundress. She held it up in front of her and gazed once more into her own anxious expression.

She knew she should be happy right now.

She knew there were a million girls out there who would gladly give their lives to be here in her place.

Give their lives . . .

Abruptly she stood up.

She crossed to the other side of the room, away from the mirror.

She didn't want to see her reflection anymore.

It looked too confused.

And too frightened.

16

iranda? You in there?"

Miranda sat up, bleary-eyed. She remembered soaking in the hot tub and slipping into a robe; she remembered picking at the lunch tray that someone had left by the bed. She even remembered lying down, but nothing at all after that.

"Miranda?" the voice called again. "It's me—Jo!"

"Come on in," Miranda answered.

"I can't. It's locked."

"Oh—sorry."

She stumbled over to open the door, and Jo poked her head in with a grin.

"Hey, where were you this morning? Robert and I played for hours, and then I couldn't find you anywhere."

"Oh . . . I just sort of hung around," Miranda hedged. "Severe jet lag, I guess. So did you win?"

"Practically." Jo laughed. "But it was a lot of fun. I really like Robert. Compared to everyone else around here, he's almost human."

"So what's Kelly doing?"

"Who knows? Every time I've seen her today, she's been wearing a new outfit. Just between you and me, I don't know why she bothers to wear anything at all. You can see practically everything she was born with." Jo stopped, considering. "And then, of course, there're those parts she *wasn't* born with, that she added later."

Miranda chuckled. "Or took off, as the case may be."

"Yes! *I* think she's had a nose job, too!"

"Well," Miranda conceded generously, "she is really pretty."

"If you say so. All set for your makeover this afternoon? Not that it's going to do *me* any good—"

"Jo, come on. It'll be fun."

"Fun to see that no makeup in the whole universe can change this particular face into a thing of beauty?"

"Stop it. You have a pretty face!"

"Do I?" Jo peered at herself in the mirror and immediately started laughing. "Maybe. If I could only find it. Somewhere beneath my eight chins!"

Miranda punched her on the shoulder. "What time do we go down?"

"About now, I think. That's why I came to get you. I can't possibly face this trauma alone."

"Then let me get dressed, and we'll suffer together."

Kelly was already there when they arrived. A maid

led them to a spacious private room at the back of the house, where Zena immediately began introducing them to hairstylists, manicurists, and cosmetologists.

"Hey, Kel!" Jo boomed, winking slyly at Miranda. "How's it going?"

Kelly shot them a withering glance and continued with her preening. Miranda and Jo climbed into their respective chairs, and the session was under way.

The afternoon proved to be a huge success. Even Jo, who'd dreaded the event, quickly got into the spirit of it, and Miranda actually found herself relaxing, forgetting the awful things that had happened that day. Sitting in her own little cubicle, pampered and fussed over by her personal team of stylists, she watched her own transformation with amazement, while Miguel snapped a step-by-step progression of photos. With a trendy new haircut and the use of a few gentle cosmetics, her own natural beauty shone forth with a radiance she'd never expected, or even imagined.

"Now!" Zena declared at last, motioning the girls from their booths. "Let us admire the stunning results!"

Amidst cheers and applause, they all stepped out, regarding one another in unconcealed delight. Kelly looked gorgeous, as Miranda had expected, but Jo was the best surprise of all. With a new layered haircut and softly defined features, she was absolutely beautiful.

"Jo, you look great," Miranda insisted, giving her friend a hug. "You really do."

Jo grinned back. "And who'd have ever thought it?"

"I mean it! I especially love your hair."

"Yeah, it's fine as long as I have Antoine here to keep fixing it. As soon as I get back home, I'll be a makeover reject."

Laughing, the two of them posed for pictures, one on each side of Kelly. Miranda could swear that Kelly actually wrinkled her nose in distaste each time one of them got a little too close.

"Don't forget dinner tonight, my dears," Zena informed them as they started back to their rooms. "And to celebrate your brand-new looks, I've had festive frocks hung in your closets."

Jo tried unsuccessfully to hide a smile. "I've always longed for a festive frock," she whispered to Miranda, and Miranda promptly elbowed her in the ribs.

"We'll meet in the foyer at seven o'clock sharp," Zena instructed them. "And since it promises to be a late night, you might want to have a little beauty rest before then. Just don't muss your hair or your face."

"See you after my beauty rest," Jo mumbled under her breath. "In my festive frock."

Swallowing a laugh, Miranda went upstairs to her room. The makeover session had been fun, but she was ready for some quiet time now, for some privacy. She locked the door and stood there for a moment, admiring her new self in the mirror. Along with the clothes that Zena had given her earlier, a brand-new dress had been carefully hung in the closet, and several pairs of shoes and handbags had been arranged on the dresser. Miranda examined everything closely, marveling once again at Zena's fashion sense, and then she undressed and eased carefully down beneath the bedcovers. She couldn't remember ever having had such an exhausting day. The traumatic events of that morning seemed distant and unreal to her now . . . and there was still so much wonderful excitement to look forward to tonight. It would feel good to relax for a while. She drifted off almost at once, and when she woke up again, felt totally refreshed.

Coincidences, she found herself thinking as she zipped up her short, strapless black dress. *Unfortunate coincidences, nothing more than that.* The statue at the pool . . . the accident with Byron's car . . . bad things happened sometimes without rhyme or reason, but now that they had, her luck was bound to change and the rest of the trip would be perfect. How could it not be? she convinced herself as she took a last approving look in the mirror. The makeover session this afternoon had done wonders at lifting her spirits—with her new dress and new look, she felt like something out of a fairy tale. And what was it that Zena had said to her earlier? *"Byron has admiring eyes for you. . . ."*

She couldn't help smiling as she brushed out her hair. She'd been so worried this morning. So anxious, so frightened—so paranoid! But that had been then, and this was now, and no more bad things were going to happen while she was here. She did a last quick appraisal of her reflection. She smiled at herself, and then she went downstairs to join the others.

They were waiting together in the entryway. Jo looked stunning in a green dress the same color as her eyes, and Kelly glowed in ice-blue satin. As Jo was exclaiming over Miranda's outfit, she suddenly frowned and grabbed her by the wrist.

"Where's your corsage?" Jo demanded.

"What corsage?"

"Byron sent us flowers," Kelly informed her. "Don't tell me you didn't get any?"

"Go look in your room," Jo urged. "It's probably there, and you just didn't see it."

Miranda nodded and started up the staircase. "Wait for me, then. I'll be right back."

It took only a moment to find it. As Miranda turned on the light, she spotted the small white box on the nightstand, half hidden behind the lamp. It was wrapped in white lace ribbon and trimmed with a sprig of baby's breath, and she could see that her name had been printed on it in tiny gold letters. She told herself that Byron hadn't really picked it out for her—he'd be much too busy to ever manage that. But still . . . it *was* a nice thought, after all. . . .

Slowly she pulled the two ends of the ribbon. She slipped one fingertip beneath the flap on the box and carefully pried it loose.

The box was filled with white tissue paper. Soft white paper sprinkled with glittery flecks of silver and gold.

There was a little white envelope lying on top. Miranda opened it, pulled out the card, and began to read.

BYRON'S HEART BELONGS TO ME.

Miranda gazed at the message with a puzzled frown.

A slow, cold chill began to build inside her.

She peeled back the top layer of tissue.

She stared down into the box.

"No . . ." she whispered. "No . . . no . . ."

Something was lying there. Something nestled deep within the folds of the white, glittery paper. Something dark, dark red, with a corsage pin stuck straight through it.

It wasn't flowers.

It was a raw, bloody heart.

17

Miranda was too horrified even to scream.

For one split second the room around her went dark—began to sway—and as she put one hand to her throat, she felt herself stagger back into the wall.

I can't faint—I can't—

I can't faint—I have a dinner to go to.

A strange sound erupted from her throat, and Miranda realized she'd laughed out loud. *I have a dinner to go to!* It was such a ridiculous thought, she knew, but the best she could manage right now under the circumstances. Laughing again, she plopped down on the edge of the bed and stared at the horrible box which she'd flung back onto the nightstand.

A heart. There's a heart in that box.

Definitely not a human heart, she tried to convince herself—it didn't look large enough for a human heart, but it was still fairly large.

She felt sick inside. As if she might throw up at any second. As if she might pass out, as if she might scream, as if she might go into hysterics if someone didn't take that box out of here right now.

In one split second her conversation with Byron came back to her again—her own words, echoing over and over now in her mind—*"Maybe it's someone close to you—maybe it's someone right here in the house—"*

But no, Byron had said, Byron had *insisted,* and he'd been almost angry at the mere suggestion of it, these are my friends, he'd said, these are people I trust. . . .

But you'd better not, Byron! she wanted to scream at him now. *You'd better not trust anyone—*

"Miranda?"

A knock sounded at the door, and Miranda jumped to her feet. She looked wildly at the door as it started to open—she looked back at the box on the nightstand. Should she tell someone? Her mind raced frantically, and she snatched the box up in her hands. Should she tell someone what was happening? *No—I've got to tell Byron first—I've got to tell Byron before I say anything to anyone—*

She didn't know what to do. She simply stood there with the box clutched in her hands, staring in horror at that door opening wider and wider. . . .

Without thinking, Miranda ran into the bathroom. She crushed the lid down on the box and tossed it into the wastebasket. A split second later Peg came tentatively into the bedroom.

"Miranda?"

"Yes?" Miranda appeared in the bathroom doorway. She shook water from her hands and dried them off with a towel.

Peg regarded her with a slight frown. "We're all waiting for you. Did you find your corsage?"

"Uh . . ." Miranda glanced around the room, shaking her head. "No. I couldn't find it anywhere."

"That Nick!" Peg burst out, exasperated. "He should have brought it up hours ago. Do I have to do everything around here myself if I want it done right?"

Miranda stared at her. "Nick?" she echoed softly. "Was Nick supposed to deliver it?"

"Yes, but as usual, he's managed to screw it up. I do apologize, Miranda. I'll make sure you get another one."

"Please don't bother. I really don't mind."

"Don't be silly. All I have to do is make a phone call. In the meanwhile, we'd better get going. We don't want to be late."

Peg turned back toward the hallway. When Miranda didn't follow, she paused on the threshold and glanced quizzically over her shoulder.

"Miranda, do you feel all right?"

"Sure. I feel great. Let's go."

After another suspicious look, Peg led the way downstairs. Miranda trailed behind, holding tight to the railing, willing herself not to fall. Who could have done such a thing? And why? And then, as another thought struck her, she froze right there in the middle of the stairs.

"Getting to you is just another way of getting to me."

Byron's words came back to her, as clearly as she'd heard them that morning at the cabin. She hadn't really believed him—hadn't *wanted* to believe him—but now . . . after everything else that had happened . . . and now *this*—

Starstruck must be close by. She must really be watching. . . .

"Miranda, are you sure you're okay?"

She hadn't been paying attention. She'd started down the steps again and hadn't noticed Peg stopping just ahead of her. As the two of them collided, Miranda jolted back to attention and apologized, while the others yelled at her to hurry up.

The limo was waiting at the front door, and to Miranda's surprise, Nick was decked out in full regalia tonight. In his uniform and cap, he looked startlingly handsome—even Kelly scrutinized him with a suggestive smile. As he helped Miranda into the car, he bowed deeply from the waist and flashed her that irresistible grin.

"You look great," he whispered in her ear. "The best one here."

"Thanks for the corsage," she mumbled.

Nick looked blank. She saw his eyes dart automatically from one corsage to another before turning back to her.

"What are you talking about?" he asked. "How come you're not wearing yours?"

"Because she didn't get one," Peg said, approaching Nick with an icy stare.

"But . . ." Nick stopped and stared at Peg. He

pushed back the brim of his cap and slowly scratched his head. "What do you mean, she didn't get one? I could have sworn I—"

"Never mind," Miranda said quickly, but Nick was rambling on.

"The guy delivered them, and I checked out all the names. I know yours was there. I mean, I *thought* it was there. No—I'm pretty sure it was there."

"Then why wasn't it in her room?" Peg demanded.

"Do I look like room service? I'm a driver, not a porter—ask whoever delivered them, don't ask me."

Grumbling under his breath, Nick slammed the door, just missing the hem of Peg's skirt. As Peg swore at him, he plopped into the front seat, turned up the radio, and pushed the accelerator to the floor.

Miranda was scarcely aware of the ride. While everyone around her laughed and chatted, eagerly anticipating the evening ahead, all she could think of was the horrible discovery she'd made in her bedroom. She didn't even notice that they'd finally reached their destination. Only when she heard excited shouting and saw people lined up on both sides of the street did she realize they were at the club.

"What are they doing here?" Nick groaned. "Who let it slip that Byron would show tonight?"

"Now, now, a little adoration never hurt anyone," Peg soothed him.

"Why do they call it the Calendar Club?" Kelly asked, arranging her tight skirt carefully over her hips.

Nick glanced back at her in the mirror. "Because you can always get a date here."

Kelly stared at him. "I don't get it."

"Calendar?" Nick prompted. "Date? Date on a calendar?"

"Oh! I get it now. That's really funny."

"Not half as funny as her brain," Jo mumbled to Miranda. "Is the great Byron Slater really supposed to meet us here, or do we dine without him?"

"Well, if he's *not* here, we just might have a riot on our hands," Miranda replied.

"Okay, Nick," Peg said brightly. "Smile for the cameras, girls."

The minute Nick jumped out and flung open their door, flashbulbs began popping like mad. Peg got out, and then Kelly, but Miranda froze where she was, staring out fearfully at the jostling crowds. Jo threw her a look of near panic. Nick reached in and practically dragged her out.

"Come on!" he yelled. "You can't eat in the backseat! You have to go inside!"

Miranda held up a hand, fending off the glare of the cameras. Kelly was actually posing and talking to some reporters.

"Look!" someone shouted. "It's a limo! They must be somebody!"

"Yeah!" another echoed. "I've seen them on TV! Hey, aren't you that girl on that soap opera?"

Miranda just managed to duck as someone grabbed for her arm. Jo let out a yelp as someone yanked her hair. Kelly giggled and began signing autographs.

"Kelly who?" someone yelled. "What movie are you in?"

"Oh, my God, I think I'm going to pass out," Jo said breathlessly. Miranda took her arm and looked wildly around for help. Nick suddenly appeared out of nowhere and hustled them both inside.

Byron was waiting for them in a private room. As Miranda glimpsed him through the doorway, she also saw Robert, Harley, and Zena all seated leisurely around a huge table. Her heart was racing, and her knees felt like rubber. She could still hear the shouts of the crowd ringing in her ears, and she reached out shakily for a glass of water.

"Are you okay?" she asked Jo.

Her friend looked up from the chair she'd collapsed into. "I don't know. Am I still alive?"

"I think so."

"Great. Then I guess I'm okay."

Miranda sat down beside her. "A person could really get killed out there."

"Yes, indeed. This is definitely the lifestyle for me."

Miranda passed Jo her glass of water. Byron was deep in conversation with Peg, but his eyes sought Miranda out across the room. She felt them the moment they touched her—felt their burning intensity and admiration. She gazed helplessly back at him. She wanted to tell him what had happened at the house, about the corsage box and its horrible contents—yet she knew this wasn't the time or the place. She'd have to keep it to herself all evening. She'd have to hold it in, the whole time she was thinking about it.

She suddenly realized she'd been staring at Byron—staring at him and worrying, without really seeing him. She brought herself sharply back to the present, and saw him lift his glass in a silent toast. He was wearing a black tuxedo with a cream-colored shirt, and his hair gleamed softly in the glow of the wall sconces.

"Okay, Miguel," Byron announced suddenly, his eyes still on Miranda. "No pictures once the entrée gets here. My guests can't enjoy dinner with flash-bulbs going off in their faces. Fair?"

Miguel and the other photographers good-naturedly agreed, and amidst the flashing of cameras, servers began bringing out trays and trays of hors d'oeuvres.

Miranda tried her best to concentrate on the festivities, to participate in the small talk going on around her. She struggled valiantly through appetizers, soup, and salad, forcing down every mouthful, yet she felt as if she were watching herself and everyone else from a long distance away. At one point she was startled to see Nick at the opposite end of the table, making faces at her over the rim of his water goblet, until Byron jabbed him in the side with his elbow and promptly sent him into a fit of coughing.

"Oh, Nick!" Zena lifted her voice above the general hubbub. "You sound absolutely consumptive, my darling. Which reminds me, Byron—I hear they're doing yet another remake of Chopin's tragic life. Perhaps it's a career move you should consider, my love—a nice little period piece for a change.

Audiences are always ripe for romance. *And* tragedy."

"Where've you been my whole career, Zena?" Byron returned with amusement. "My films already have about all the romance and tragedy an audience can stand."

"And what sort of action vehicle would that be exactly?" Robert teased Zena. "A runaway piano? Or—I know—maybe some terrorists *hijack* his piano? Or maybe Chopin's really an undercover agent who can kickbox his way out of—"

"Enough, enough!" Zena waved her arms impatiently as everyone laughed. "You simply do not appreciate true creativity! You simply do not appreciate true art!"

"True art and creativity seldom make money," Peg said with a wry smile.

"And God knows how we all appreciate money," Robert replied, deadpan.

Again everyone laughed, and Miranda made an effort to join in. God, how she wished the dinner would be over! As the main course arrived, she watched in fear as servers came in to remove the silver covers from the plates. All she could see was that little white box and the bloody red thing inside it. And as her waiter put her own plate down in front of her, she was terrified for him to lift off the cover. . . .

Miranda sighed. It was just some nouveau concoction—a fancy presentation and very little *real* food. She could relax a bit. The conversation blurred around her. She let her gaze drift from one face to another. Could one of these people be responsible for the box in her room? They were all people Byron trusted—yet who *else* could have put it there? It would have been easy for any one of them to switch the box, to exchange it for the real corsage Nick swore he saw earlier. *Any one of them . . .*

Oh, Byron, I've got to talk to you. I've got to tell you what happened, I've got to warn you.

As though he'd suddenly read her mind, she saw Byron staring at her. He raised an eyebrow and smiled and kept on eating. *I'm the only one,* Miranda thought desperately. *Just Byron and now me. The only ones who really know there's danger.*

"Dangerous?" Peg spoke aloud, and Miranda snapped back to attention. "Of course it's dangerous, Kelly, it's a cutthroat business, pure and simple. You've got to stay on top of things—you've got to watch your competition every second—take every opportunity you can. If I've told Byron once—"

"You've told him—*and us*—a million times," Robert finished for her.

"You've got to be aware," Peg went on, as though Robert hadn't even spoken. "You've got to be aware of what everyone else is doing, because there's always someone waiting in the wings to pass you by."

"Of course it helps if you have your own *personal* cutthroat," Robert added amiably. "That's why we have Peg. She's so good at what she does."

"Right," Nick tossed in. "In fact, Peg graduated at the top of her class at the cutthroat academy."

Peg shot each of them an icy glance. Robert and Nick both leaned back in their chairs, exchanging triumphant grins.

"But *nobody* can compete with you, Byron." Kelly sighed loudly. "I don't know why anyone would even try."

"That's it," Jo muttered to Miranda under her breath. "This is the part where I really get sick."

Miranda nodded. "Think I'll join you."

Dessert dragged by. One lively group, the movie production assistants, decided to take in some night life, and left while coffee was being served. The rest of them continued to sit and talk until Peg finally announced that it was time to leave. Miranda had never felt so grateful in her entire life.

She followed the others to the exit, then heard Jo give a yelp of surprise. The sidewalks were even more crowded now than they'd been earlier, and as Byron appeared in the doorway, total pandemonium broke loose. Miranda had never seen anything like it. While hordes of fans pushed and shoved and screamed Byron's name, cameras exploded wildly from all directions.

"My God," Robert said, turning on Peg. "Don't these people realize how late it is? Don't they ever go home?"

For once Peg didn't have an answer. In fact, she looked every bit as shocked as the others.

"Come on," Robert said anxiously. "Out the back. Hurry!"

Miranda didn't have time to think. As everyone raced toward the rear of the club, she could feel the tension mounting, could feel the unspoken fears surrounding her on every side. Someone grabbed her hand, and she suddenly realized that Byron had ahold of her.

"When you go out the door, don't stop for anything," he directed her. "Just keep moving till you're inside the car."

"But what about you? You're the one they're after!"

"Don't worry about him," Harley said gruffly. "That's my job."

Miranda managed a nod. She saw Jo glance back at her for one brief moment before Robert pushed her forward.

"Where's Nick?" Robert demanded. "Has anyone seen Nick? Keep moving—keep moving—"

"I think he went out to get the car," Zena panted. "Didn't he, Peg? Didn't Nick go out to get the car?"

"Then he must have seen us. He's probably already pulled around back. Are we all here?" Robert paused and pressed back against the wall as everyone else streamed by. Miranda could tell he was counting noses, and she had a sudden irrational urge to laugh.

"I see him!" Peg cried. "He's just pulling up now!"

"We can't go out there!" Zena insisted. "Look! People must have seen the limo—they're all following it!"

Immediately Robert flung open the door and braced it with his shoulder. "Go!" he shouted. "Run and don't stop!"

Miranda was terrified. Before she could even think, someone was shoving her outside and she was racing across the parking lot. The noise was deafening. Shrieks and screams, shouts and sobbings—everything ran together in a thunderous roar. Her legs moved in slow motion. Her lungs felt about to burst. Arms clawed at her from every side; she fought her way through bunches of flowers, books and pens, bits of clothing, clutching hands. She was vaguely aware of someone gripping her arm, shoving her, and once she glanced back to see Byron's face ducked low and Harley angled over him as he forced his way through the mob. She could feel her body snap from side to side—could feel the sharp jerk of her clothes being torn. *We're going to die,* she thought frantically—*we're all going to die out here*—

She couldn't breathe. Hands in her hair, pulling—fists beating on her back, on her neck—shrill cries echoing in her ears—flesh being scraped from her arms. She felt as if she were suffocating, being buried alive. She tried to push the crowds away, but they surged in even closer.

"Keep going!" someone shouted. *Byron?* But she didn't know anymore, she couldn't think, she couldn't even move. For one split second she thought she saw Peg far ahead of her, waving her wildly toward the limo. Something rammed her from behind, and she tried desperately to keep from falling. She felt something land across her feet. She flailed wildly, trying to keep her balance, before the force of the crowd moved her helplessly forward again.

In a burst of panic Miranda realized that she was alone, that somehow she'd become separated from the others. She couldn't feel Byron behind her anymore; she couldn't see Harley anywhere. She tried to scream, tried to claw her way through the mob, but it was totally out of control, there was no escape.

"Help me!" she screamed, but she knew it was hopeless, she knew no one could hear her. And yet, even in that instant, she felt arms go around her, she felt someone lift her up and hold her tight, she felt herself being carried through the darkness, through the horrible insanity.

"Hold on!" Nick yelled. "I've got you!"

The next thing she knew, she was tumbling into the limo, and people were grabbing her, pulling her to safety. She thought she heard someone crying. And then there was a voice—Robert's voice calling out, "Wait! Where's Byron?"

"I don't know, I don't know," Zena moaned. "One minute he was there, and the next—"

"He was right behind me," Miranda murmured. "He was with Harley—he had ahold of my arm—"

Peg sat ramrod straight, trying to peer through the window, trying to search through the crowd. "I can't see him anywhere! Oh, God, Nick—something's happened to Byron!"

"Calm down, Peg," Robert ordered.

"You've got to go back for him. You've got to go back!"

"How can he go back?" Kelly wailed. "It's a full-scale riot out there! We're all going to be killed!"

Peg's voice rose hysterically. "This can't be happening! Where's Byron! Oh, God, Nick—*do* something! Do something before it's too—"

The piercing shriek of a siren drowned out the rest of her words. Nick glanced back at them from the front seat, throwing up his hands in despair.

"Maybe he went back inside the club."

"That's impossible," Zena fired back. "He could never have made it back the way we came. Drive, Nick!"

"Drive where? If I move an inch, I'll run over somebody! I'm going back to look for Byron."

"The cops are going crazy out there," Robert argued. "They'll never let you through." Before Nick had a chance to respond, Robert put his hand on the door. "I'm going with you. You girls stay here, and keep the doors *locked!*"

"Be careful!" Peg warned him. Her hands were shaking; her face was drained white. As Robert and Nick jumped out of the car, she slammed her fist down on the automatic lock button. For an endless moment the limo rocked from side to side as people swarmed over and around it. And then . . . at last . . . it began to settle. The noise began to fade.

Miranda kept her eyes on the smoked windows of the car. She watched as the crowd gradually calmed and drew back . . . as the police herded everyone away.

It didn't take long after that. It seemed like only minutes before Robert returned to them again, before Peg was opening the doors and reaching frantically for his outstretched arms.

"What is it?" she asked him. "What's happened?"

And Miranda was so aware of the silence . . . so very aware of the strange, heavy silence that had fallen so suddenly. Such a loud cruel silence after the deafening chaos of the crowds . . .

"It's Byron," Robert murmured.

"Oh, God!" Peg gasped. "Oh, Robert—"

"He's been hurt."

"But is he all right? Is he going to be okay?"

"Peg," he said slowly, and his eyes were calm and steady on hers. "I think we should get these girls home, don't you? They've called an ambulance and—"

"No!" Peg cried. "What are you saying, Robert? What's happened?"

Miranda's heart lodged sickeningly in her throat. She could hear Kelly crying softly in the background. She could feel Jo holding her breath.

"Byron's hurt," Robert said again. "Byron and Harley were caught in the crowd and . . ."

His words trailed away. His voice caught and began to tremble.

"It's Harley," Robert whispered. "He's dead."

18

Once more the silence fell.

Harsh and heavy and endless.

As the door opened wider and Nick leaned in behind him, Robert spoke at last.

"I don't know any details right now. Only that we've got to get Byron to the emergency room."

"I want to see him!" Peg insisted, but Robert took her firmly by the shoulders and shook his head.

"There's nothing you can do. We'll follow him to the hospital."

"Harley," Zena murmured. She leaned her head on the window glass and closed her eyes. "How can he be dead? How can this be possible?"

Robert didn't answer. Zena, with eyes still shut, spoke softly.

"This is our worst nightmare. Something we have always feared—something *every* star fears more than anything else in the world. Being injured—even killed—by his loving fans."

Miranda drew her breath in slowly. A cold knot of horror twisted deep in her stomach. *His loving fans . . .* She huddled back in the seat and groped for Jo's hand. Vaguely she realized that Kelly was squeezing her other hand.

"We should take the girls home," Robert said again. He sounded tired . . . numb. "I think that'd be best."

"I can drop them off," Nick offered, and Robert nodded.

"Yes," Peg agreed. "Yes, Nick, take them home. Everyone—just go on with the evening as planned. If Byron's injuries aren't serious, perhaps he'll join us later."

Robert and Nick exchanged glances. "Peg." Robert fixed her with a solemn look. "Harley is *dead!*"

"Yes," Peg murmured. "Yes, I know that, Robert, but these girls are not involved in this situation. They must go on. *We* must go on."

"Jesus, Peg, you are really and truly nuts." Nick sighed, while Robert backed away from her, his voice going slightly incredulous.

"We've had a tragedy here, Peg. This is hardly the time for business as usual!"

"But the contest . . ." Peg sat there stiff and straight. *Like a wax dummy,* Miranda thought. *Like someone who's not even real.* "The winners . . . the week with Byron Slater . . ."

"It's over," Robert announced firmly. He reached in, pulled Peg and Zena from the car, then prodded

Nick into the front seat, slamming both doors behind them. "I'll get us a cab. Go on, Nick."

Nick gave a quick salute and immediately sped away.

It was quite a different atmosphere on the way home. None of the laughter or conversation or eager expectations that they'd all shared earlier that night on their way to the club. The girls were quiet, lost in their own thoughts. Nick kept his eyes purposefully on the road, and they all avoided looking at one another. Miranda was relieved when the ride was finally over and they were back at the estate once again.

"I've got to get back," Nick said awkwardly as he ushered them into the foyer. "I don't know what to say to you guys. It wasn't—" He broke off, biting his lip. He shook his head and tried again. "It wasn't supposed to be like this."

Miranda felt sorry for him. The devil-may-care attitude had vanished; he looked stunned and incredibly sad. *But of course he's sad,* Miranda reminded herself. *Harley's dead, Nick's lost a friend. They've all lost a friend. And no one even knows for sure how Byron is. . . .*

"Well . . . see you."

Nick turned on his heel and walked back outside, leaving the three of them uncertainly in the hallway.

"I don't feel like doing anything," Jo mumbled. "I just want to get out of here."

Miranda managed some vague reply. Even Kelly had lost her luster.

Kelly sighed. "Well, we can't leave till tomorrow. So what do we do in the meantime? I'd really like to know what's going on with Byron." As the other two nodded in agreement, she added, "And I don't really want to go to my room, either. To tell you the truth . . . I don't feel like being alone just now."

Jo stared at her. Kelly offered a tentative smile, and Jo smiled back.

"Me, neither," Jo admitted. "I can't believe any of this, you know? It really *was* like a nightmare. One of those horrible ones where you run and run, but you can't wake up."

"I thought I was going to die," Miranda murmured, and then wished she hadn't said it. The other two stared at her, and she thought guiltily of Harley.

"How could it happen?" Kelly asked them. "With everything so glamorous and so wonderful—how could something like this happen?"

Miranda shook her head. Her mind was whirling, yet it felt strangely paralyzed. She couldn't think anymore—didn't *want* to think anymore. As from a long distance off she heard Jo make a cautious suggestion.

"Maybe we *should* see that film. At least it'll keep our minds off everything else. At least till everyone gets back and we hear something."

"Why did Peg want us to see this film anyway?" Miranda gave her a quizzical look. "Does anyone know?"

"I do," Kelly volunteered. "She said everyone expects it to be the latest sleeper, and she wanted our opinion of it."

"What does *our* opinion matter?" Jo snorted. "Is Byron in it?"

"No, it's a couple of new actors nobody's ever

heard of. But Peg said Byron's watched it a lot and thinks it's really going to take off." Kelly hesitated, then glanced from Jo to Miranda. "Do you think Byron will be all right?"

Jo shrugged her shoulders. "I don't know. I hope so."

They found a maid who directed them to the private theater. As they settled back in the comfortably plush seats, Miranda was grateful for the darkness. She didn't want the others to see the worry on her face, the tears in her eyes. Because ever since they'd left the club—ever since she'd heard the news about Byron—one brutal, relentless thought had been pounding in her head, ripping at her heart.

What if it wasn't an accident! What if someone was deliberately trying to kill Byron and got Harley by mistake!

She tried to think back, back to her panic and terror in the crowd. Who had been there, so close to Byron? People's faces were a total blur—the crowd had been like one heaving monster to her, not like separate individuals at all.

But who of *Byron's* people had been there? Close to him, within reach of him?

Stop this, she told herself firmly. *You don't even know what happened to Byron—you don't even know how Harley died.* And yet she *couldn't* stop it, she couldn't stop that one fearful possibility from playing itself out in her head. . . .

She thought hard, trying to reconstruct the scene again in her mind. All of them had been close, she realized at last—all of them had been bunched together at first, like so many cattle to the slaughterhouse, fighting their way through the frenzied mob. All of them had run from the club, all of them ringed around Byron—all of them close enough to touch him, to do him harm.

She closed her eyes and drew a deep breath.

But what if, after all, it really *wasn't* any of them? What if, after all, it really was some anonymous female fan who'd been stalking him, watching him, all this time? How simple to slip through a crowd unnoticed! How easy to hit your target and be off again, quickly and silently, with no one the wiser! Nobody would have noticed her or anything about her—nobody would have seen or heard a thing. If there'd been the slightest struggle or sound at all, the rioting of the crowd would have drowned them completely out. Harley himself had probably not even known. One minute he'd been pressed close to Byron, guarding him, protecting him, and the next minute . . .

Harley's dead.

Miranda opened her eyes again and stared blindly at the big screen. She had no idea what this stupid movie was about, or even who was in it. The last thing she could possibly care about right now was some ridiculous film.

You've got to stop this. You're letting your mind go wild, you're jumping to crazy conclusions, you're blowing things way out of proportion. Byron probably fell, and that's all. Harley probably died by accident. . . .

Oh, Byron, if only I could talk to you now, if only you could tell me . . .

Byron right next to her, Byron steering her

through the crowd. She thought of the heart in the corsage box, and the note in there with it, and just remembering it again turned the blood cold in her veins.

And perhaps Byron really *hadn't* been the target of the attack after all, she found herself speculating. Maybe not Byron at all . . .

She recalled now how he'd fallen against her, how Harley had stumbled on top of Byron, how she'd very nearly been pushed down beneath the waving, stomping masses of arms and legs and feet. Perhaps *that's* when the attack had happened, she suddenly realized—right then with Byron so close beside her.

And perhaps *she* had been the target of the attack.

And in the pushing, shoving crowd, the weapon had somehow just missed its mark. . . .

BYRON'S HEART BELONGS TO ME. . . .

And Starstruck wouldn't let anyone get in her way.

19

The others returned just after the movie ended. The screen had gone blank, the lights had come up, and the girls continued to sit in their seats, trying to keep up a conversation, trying to keep their minds on anything but reality.

They all agreed the movie was terrible; they all agreed they couldn't have been less interested. There was a buffet set up afterward, but none of them was hungry. As they sat there in the theater, Peg showed up at last, saying she had news from the hospital.

"Byron's going to be fine," she informed them. There was an audible sigh of relief, and grateful looks were exchanged all around. "He's got some cuts and bruises," Peg went on, "and they're keeping him overnight for observation."

She was like a different person now, Miranda noticed. All brusqueness and business. Miranda decided she liked the other Peg better—the one who'd actually shown some honest emotion for maybe two whole minutes.

"Then," Jo ventured cautiously, "is Harley really . . ."

Peg gave a curt nod. "Yes. We don't have the results back from the doctor yet. We should hear more tomorrow."

The girls didn't know what to say. Somehow it seemed more real to them now . . . more final. As Miranda continued staring at Peg, she noticed the dark circles beneath her eyes, the whiteness of her lips. Maybe Peg was human after all, Miranda thought to herself. Under closer scrutiny that polished veneer looked as if it just might be starting to crack.

"That's all the information I have now, girls," Peg said tightly. "I'm asking you to please refrain from talking to the press—actually, not to say anything to anyone about what's happened here tonight. I've prepared a statement, which Robert is giving now by the front gates. It's a simple matter for the media to find out your names, and they'll probably try to question you. May I remind you that it would be in Byron's best interest if you refuse."

As one, the girls nodded.

"I've spoken with Byron at length, and he asked me to convey his deepest regrets to you. We're all aware of how badly things have turned out tonight. On behalf of Byron—and all of us—I can only say how very sorry I am."

Miranda could see Kelly's lip trembling. Jo's face was lowered and grave.

"Well," Peg concluded. "Maybe we should all try to get some sleep for now. I'll have more information for you in the morning."

Surprised, Miranda glanced over at Jo, who was looking back at her with the same baffled expression. Peg hadn't said a word about them leaving. Maybe with everything else on her mind, she'd simply forgotten to mention it. Or maybe, Miranda decided, that would come up in the morning, with the rest of Peg's update.

She accompanied the others back to the foyer, then stood watching as they headed off to the guesthouse. She didn't want to go back to her own room. She had no desire to be anywhere near that wastebasket, to touch the box again, to see its grisly contents. For a long time she simply stood there in the entryway, then finally dragged herself upstairs. She opened her door and paused on the threshold. After a long while she went into the bathroom and looked down into the trash.

The wastebasket was empty.

The box was gone.

20

Miranda stared down in confusion.

Had someone taken it? The idea seemed preposterous, yet she was sure the box had been there when she'd left for dinner. She'd wanted to save it for Byron—to show it to him so he could have proof—to show everyone else so they'd believe him.

How could it have disappeared?

Shaken, Miranda walked out onto the balcony. Even from this distance she could hear shouts and upraised voices coming from the front gates, she could see flashbulbs bursting against the night sky. The media was out for blood, too, she guessed. *Just like Starstruck . . .*

Yet Peg hadn't mentioned any sort of foul play. And Byron's injuries seemed minor enough. Maybe it really *was* an accident, Miranda puzzled. *Maybe*

I really am letting my imagination run away with me. . . .

She thought about the possibility of going home tomorrow. She thought about the contest and the female lead and Byron's new film. How could the contest possibly mean anything to any of them now? Harley was dead, and Byron was lying injured in the hospital. The whole experience had been tainted somehow. Tonight's incident had cast a dark shadow over the whole trip.

She let her eyes wander over the roofline . . . the foliage clustered thick below her . . . the silhouettes of outbuildings that showed through the trees. She could see a light in the upstairs window of the garage, and she wondered what Nick was doing, what Nick was thinking at this very minute. Jo and Kelly would go back home without the slightest clue of what had been going on around here. Of what had been going on all this time, behind the picture-perfect facade of this picture-perfect estate.

Miranda sighed and closed her eyes. She leaned her head against the wall, and then suddenly, slowly, she became aware of voices talking nearby—voices low and urgent and deep in conversation. It began to occur to her that they must be coming from another balcony very close to her own, but obscured by the angles of the outside walls. She opened her eyes again and leaned forward. It wasn't that she really *meant* to eavesdrop, exactly—it was just that the hard tone of Peg's voice precluded any sort of secrecy.

"I'm *not* going to cause a panic, do you understand? These girls are here for a good time, and I'll be *damned* if I let anything ruin their fun!"

"You don't care about their fun! All you care about is keeping this thing quiet!"

"And is that so terrible of me, that I don't want the wrong kind of publicity! Studios are funny about things like that, Robert—or have you forgotten? They might say he's jinxed, that he's too big a risk! We have to think about his career!"

"I thought *you* were supposed to be thinking about it. If Byron's dead, there *is* no career!"

"I'll work it out. I'll make it sound completely believable. I mean, this sort of thing could happen in any kind of crowd. There's no need to make an issue of it. You and I both know that Harley's family had a history of heart trouble—"

"*Family* history, Peg. The guy was as strong as a horse."

"But no one knows any different, so that's what we'll tell people. That it was merely a heart attack."

"It *wasn't* a heart attack. Harley was *stabbed!* Harley was *killed,* for God's—!"

"We can keep it quiet!" Peg insisted. "Just for a while, just until the initial shock passes. No one can prove it was deliberate, anyway. And until that *can* be proved, it's still an accident, pure and simple. Overzealous fans in an overzealous crowd. Unintentional and most unfortunate. Harley gave his life defending his boss—something to that effect. We'll turn Harley into a hero!"

"That's not going to matter to Harley now—that's not going to bring him back or fix what's wrong here!

Why not tell the truth? Why won't you admit that Byron's in danger?"

"Because he's *not* in danger!" Peg exploded furiously. "Two silly phone calls, Robert. That *hardly* constitutes a death threat."

"And what about his car?"

"Oh, for God's sake, *Nick* takes care of the cars. It's a wonder we *all* haven't been killed before now, as incompetent as Nick is."

"Nick's a natural-born mechanic, and you know it."

"Nick's totally worthless. *That's* what I know."

"All right, then what about the autograph book? You saw it yourself when Byron showed it to us—"

"I saw words on paper. Nothing more."

"Then how did it get into Byron's study?"

"Oh, Robert, how the hell should I know? The thing is, how do we choose to *react* to it? We've got plenty of protection—"

"Protection! Byron's best protection just got himself killed tonight—"

"—and the best thing to do is ignore it. If we give it media attention, it will just encourage this person, whoever she may be. That's how these fiendish minds work, don't you understand? Giving her attention will only encourage her to come up with bigger and better threats—just to wallow in her own publicity! I won't be a party to that. No. I certainly won't."

"And since when have you become such an expert on sociopathic behavior? You can't keep wraps on this forever—one of these days it's going to get out, Peg. But then it might be too late!"

"And I'm telling you one more time, it's absolutely *not* worth calling negative attention to—"

"Peg"—Robert sighed in desperation—"as Byron's agent, I must insist—"

"Oh, shut up, Robert, you don't know what you're dealing with here!" Peg snapped back at him. *"I* know what's best for Byron! *I* know what the public will and won't accept much better than you do."

"What's that supposed to mean?"

"It means your friendship with Byron is clouding your judgment."

"My friendship?" Robert returned mildly. "Well, it's not like I've ever slept with him or anything, is it, Peg? Not like I've ever been dumped by him? Or been jealous of all his other girlfriends?"

The silence was lethal and dangerous. Miranda could picture Peg's tight-lipped expression, and the glare of pure hatred in her eyes.

"I made Byron what he is today," Peg seethed. "Whether you want to admit it or not. Not you, Robert—*me!* Byron owes everything to me. *Everything!"*

"Everything?" Robert repeated softly. "Even his life?"

21

Miranda slept fitfully.

She tossed and turned, but her dreams were full of writhing bodies that collapsed on top of her, burying her alive. Through a smoky haze she saw Byron glancing over his shoulder—saw his quick look of shock and terror—saw him reaching out to her as she ran away. In agonizing detail she saw Harley starting to fall, heard him shouting for help, even as he was being trampled mercilessly by the mob.

"Run, Miranda!"

Byron's lips moving, trying to warn me—a black veiled figure with a knife—"Run, Miranda, she wants to kill you—leave now! Leave while you still can!"

Miranda sat up, gasping for breath.

Her heart was hammering out of control, and a scream stuck in her throat. She looked down and realized she was clutching the covers in panic.

187

Only a nightmare . . . only a horrible dream . . .

Night sounds floated softly in to her. Soft wind . . . soft warmth . . . the soft rustling of trees . . . the soft fragrance of flowers.

Miranda frowned.

A nightmare . . . but it had seemed so real. . . .

She shifted a little in the bed. The covers stirred gently around her, and shadows slid across the walls. *A movie,* she thought dreamily. *I feel as if I'm in a scene from a movie. . . .*

"Leave, Miranda . . . leave now . . . leave while you still can. . . ."

The dream was gone, yet the voice still echoed stubbornly in her head. Like the voice of a kindly phantom, like the voice of some guardian angel . . .

There was a faint whisper of air. The curtains moved and settled at the four corners of the bed, and Miranda turned immediately toward the French doors.

"Is someone there?" she called in alarm.

But of course no one was there, she told herself firmly. *What's wrong with you anyway? You're all alone in here, just you and what's left of your stupid bad dream.*

And yet something *was* wrong.

Something was very wrong, and she could feel it deep, deep in her heart.

She sat there a moment, trying to collect her thoughts, peering into the darkness, eyes adjusting slowly to the gloom. Just the faintest glow of silver shone through the half-open doors of the balcony.

The room *seemed* normal. Nothing out of place that she could recall. And yet . . .

Cautiously she swung her feet to the carpet and inched over toward the French doors. Pulling the curtains a little, she gazed out onto the deserted balcony, then let out a sigh of relief.

Miranda, what is wrong with you? I really think you're losing your mind.

She turned back around. She put her hands to her forehead and rubbed the dull ache behind her eyes. Just the aftermath of a nightmare, she told herself firmly. Nothing more than that.

And yet she *knew* what was bothering her. It wasn't the dream, exactly, it was the *voice* in the dream. The voice trying to warn her, the voice urging her to get away.

The voice coming from Byron's mouth, and yet strangely enough, it hadn't sounded at all like Byron. That's what it was, she realized now—Byron's voice, yet *not* Byron's voice.

But it *was* a voice she recognized.

Miranda frowned and tried to remember.

A voice telling her to leave . . .

It had sounded so real in the dream—so *real!* Almost as if it hadn't been a dream at all . . .

Don't be silly. Of course it was a dream. What else could it have been?

She sighed and hugged her arms around her chest. She shivered uneasily, and her eyes went once more around the room, nervously inspecting each corner, the closet, the open door to the bathroom.

And then she glanced over at the side of her bed.

And she realized she hadn't noticed it before because it was so *close* to the bed, because she'd probably stepped right over it on her way to the balcony. . . .

In the plush carpet there was just the faintest sprinkling of grass. As though maybe it had come from the bottom of a shoe.

Miranda frowned and tried to think back. They hadn't been anywhere grassy tonight—they'd only walked on floors and concrete and pavement. . . .

So where had the grass come from?

Again her eyes made a slow search of the room. Again a chill crawled through her.

That voice in the dream . . . sounding so real.

"Leave now, Miranda, leave now . . ."

That voice sounding so real because maybe it *was* real, Miranda realized with a shock.

And whoever had spoken to her had been standing right here, right here beside her pillow, right here beside her bed.

22

"Harley had a weak heart," Peg said solemnly. "We'd known about it for some time, but we never thought—"

She broke off, with a perfect catch in her voice, a perfect glimmer of tears in her eyes. Kelly and Jo and Lucille and the others looked sad and stricken at the news.

"He gave his life for Byron," Peg went on sadly. "They were such good friends, so very close. Harley would have wanted it that way. Byron, as you can imagine, is devastated."

She stopped, drew a deep breath. Miranda sat at the table watching her and felt hatred, pure and simple, welling up inside.

"I'm afraid he'll have to remain in the hospital a few more days—only a few, mind you—just until he's better able to cope with this tragedy. But in the meantime, Byron has insisted—has *begged* me—to see that this week continues as planned. That all of you enjoy the things we promised you'd enjoy."

Kelly's smile was a mixture of happiness and relief. Jo glanced at Miranda and looked gravely uncomfortable. As they all got up from the briefing and started their separate ways, Jo leaned over and touched Miranda's arm.

"Look," Jo said, "I really don't feel like staying here anymore. I don't think it's right to hang around after what's happened."

"What are you saying?" Kelly burst out. "It'd be rude of us to leave now, if Byron *wants* us to stay!"

"Kelly's right." Peg walked up to them with a professional smile. "It would make Byron feel even *worse* if he thought he'd ruined your good time. So for *Byron's* sake, I *insist* that you girls stay. Seeing you happy will make Byron even happier."

Miranda glanced over at Robert. He'd been sitting at the other side of the table all this time, arms folded over his chest, eyes fixed on his untouched breakfast. She heard him clear his throat. He wouldn't even look at Peg.

"The personal dangers that a star like Byron must face are astronomical," Peg went on. "But it's the price he pays for his public. They love him so very much, they often don't realize how they can harm him, too."

She rested one hand on Kelly's shoulder. She gave her a sympathetic pat.

"When this sort of accident happens, it reminds all of us just how vulnerable our celebrities really are. This senseless tragedy should never have happened, and I hope to God it *never* happens to someone else. I just hope you girls can put this unpleasant incident out of your minds. We thought a shopping spree on Rodeo Drive might lift your spirits a little."

Jo hadn't taken her eyes from Miranda's face. Now her eyebrows lifted in disbelief, and Miranda stared back at her in shared amazement. Even Kelly looked uncertain, glancing from Jo to Miranda and back again.

"I'm afraid Robert and I have a million things to take care of," Peg went on, "so Zena will accompany you today. If you need anything at all, don't hesitate to ask her or Nick."

At the mention of Nick's name, Miranda glanced quickly around the room. She hadn't seen him since he'd dropped them off last night, and she wondered how he'd react to this latest turn of events.

After promising to meet again in half an hour, the girls went off to their rooms. Miranda managed to find a maid working in the upstairs hall and stopped her with a question.

"Excuse me, but I was wondering about the trash can in my bathroom?"

"Yes, miss. Does it need to be emptied?" the maid asked obligingly.

"No, I was just wondering how often you *do* empty it."

"Every evening, miss. The trash goes out every single night from every single room of the house. Is there a problem?"

"No. No problem. Thanks a lot."

The maid smiled and went back to her cleaning,

and Miranda went back to her room. She'd never get to show Byron that corsage box now—she didn't even know when she'd be able to talk to him. She wished desperately that she could confide in someone else—that she had someone to share her fears and suspicions with. She didn't feel right about involving Jo, and Kelly was out of the question. Lucille's business was gossip, so she wouldn't do at all. Robert seemed like a good friend to Byron, but right now he had his hands full with other things and was much too accessible to Peg. Nick? Nick had befriended her from the very beginning. He seemed genuinely concerned about Byron, and the two of them had a history together—but hadn't Lucille mentioned something about bad feelings between them once?

Forget it, Miranda told herself. *You can't tell a soul.*

Who could she trust, really? And to confide in *anyone* would be breaking her pact with Byron—something she simply couldn't bring herself to do.

Zena was the only one who talked on the way into town. Lucille and Miguel seemed preoccupied with their own thoughts; even Nick was uncharacteristically quiet. As he maneuvered the limo through busy streets, Miranda peered curiously out the window. She'd always heard about the famous Rodeo Drive, yet she still wasn't prepared for what awaited them when they got there.

The place was absolutely packed. Shoppers and tourists thronged the walkways, and Nick braced their door against a steady flow of people while Zena herded them all out. Giorgio . . . Armani . . .

Chanel . . . They were all there, row after row of famous shops, boutiques, and designer fashions. Restaurants and bistros and sidewalk cafés. From time to time one of the girls recognized a famous face—and then there were those who only looked as though they *should* be famous.

Zena, although greatly subdued today, was still very much in her element. As she made her rounds with the girls, she called everyone by name, hugged every single salesperson, and was generally treated like visiting royalty. At every store, Miranda and her companions were fussed over and photographed, then ushered into private rooms, where each was catered to by an individual dresser—"Chosen just for you, my precious darling!" Zena delighted in informing them. And even though Miranda had made up her mind that she'd *never* be able to enjoy this day in a million years, she actually found herself getting into the swing of things. Item after item of expensive clothing was handpicked, charged to Lucille's *On the Edge* credit card, boxed, bagged, and hangered, then handed over to a very bored-looking Nick, who loitered outside and uncomplainingly stuffed package after package into the limousine.

They stopped for lunch at a swank restaurant, and Zena kept them entertained the whole time, spotting various movie stars and calling them by name. Several even stopped by their table to chat, and on more than one occasion, Miranda thought Kelly was going to faint.

After lunch there was more shopping, more clothes, more pampering, only this time with a bevy of photographers following them every step of the way. By midafternoon Miranda's feet felt numb, and as the others headed into the last boutique, she begged off, insisting she had to get something to drink before she died of thirst.

"Are you sure?" Zena worried. "You haven't even seen all these wonderful clothes in here, my sweetness—"

"I'll come right back," Miranda promised. "Just give me a minute to rest."

"I'll go with her," Nick spoke up quickly, and Zena looked relieved.

"Yes, Nick, you go and take good care of her, won't you? And bring her back to us, relaxed and refreshed!"

Nick gave his usual salute, then took Miranda's arm and propelled her down the sidewalk.

"You look a little done in," he admitted, steering her toward an open-air café.

"I *am* done in. I've decided I can never be a movie star. I couldn't stand all the stress of being spoiled."

"Yeah, well, it's a tough life, you know?" Nick grinned again and pulled her chair out with a flourish. "May I make a recommendation?"

"Recommend away."

"The cherry Cokes here are the best in the world. I think you'd hate yourself if you went home without trying one."

"Well, I wouldn't want to have any regrets." Miranda smiled at him, and Nick promptly gave the waitress their order and sat down across from her at the little table.

"So." Nick folded his arms on the tabletop and

leaned toward her. He wasn't smiling anymore. His voice softened, and he kept his eyes down. "The week of your dreams, right?"

Miranda shook her head. "How is Byron, really? Do you know?"

"Maybe you should ask Peg," Nick returned. "She seems to have all the answers for everything."

"It's just that I can't stop thinking about what happened last night. Poor Harley. I . . ."

Miranda's words trailed off. She wanted so desperately to voice her suspicions, to talk them over with somebody else. She wished Nick would say something—anything—to reassure her.

"It's strange," she heard herself mumbling.

"What is?"

"How everyone's just going on. How Zena's still taking us shopping, and you and I are sitting here having something to drink. And the whole time we're all doing these things, Harley's dead. And Byron's in the hospital because . . ."

Again she trailed off. She saw a frown on Nick's brow—she saw him lean even closer.

"You and I both know something, Miranda," he said softly. "Don't we."

Miranda's eyes widened in surprise. The waitress brought their drinks and set them down on the table between them.

"Two cherry Cokes. Anything else?" she offered.

When Nick didn't answer, the woman scribbled a ticket and left it beside his glass. Nick mumbled a thank-you, then took a long sip through his straw.

"What are you talking about?" Miranda tried to sound casual.

"You know what I'm talking about. And you probably also know that Peg's not telling everything." Nick looked up at her then. He tipped his glass . . . chewed thoughtfully on some ice. "Byron told me he was *pushed* last night. That he sensed something was wrong when Harley fell on him—that he had this panicky feeling that something bad was happening."

Miranda felt herself nodding. Nick's frown deepened as he twirled his straw between his fingers.

"Byron said there wasn't anything he could do," Nick added. "When you're trapped in a crowd like that, you could get crushed in a heartbeat, and nobody would ever know. I've been in situations like that with him before. And believe me, it's damn scary."

"I do believe you," Miranda insisted. "I was terrified last night. I've never felt so helpless."

"Byron said it was a fan who shoved him."

Miranda's pulse quickened. Nick was peering at her intently, as though gauging her response.

"Well, of course it *would* be a fan, Nick. I mean, the crowd was *full* of fans—"

"Look." Nick's tone was serious. "I like you, Miranda, you're a smart girl. Too smart to get mixed up emotionally with someone like Byron. You don't belong in this world of his, and I don't want to see you get hurt."

Miranda regarded him in surprise. "Meaning?" she replied coolly.

"Meaning, from what I've seen, it seems like the two of you have something starting here, and I want to save you from a disaster."

"Well, thank you very much, but like I told you before, I really can take care of myself."

"No, wait." Nick reached out for her arm as she started to get up. "Just hear me out."

"Why should I?"

"Because you need to know what I'm thinking."

"Actually, I think I need to get back."

"Wait," Nick said again. His hold tightened around her arm, and Miranda sank slowly back in her chair.

"First off," Nick began, "I think Byron should go away. Farther than Italy. Longer than two weeks. For a really long rest. Till things calm down and get figured out. I think he needs to be away from here and especially away from Peg. This crazy life clouds your judgment, messes up your mind."

"What are you talking about?"

Nick hesitated. His grip relaxed on Miranda's arm, and he pulled his hand away.

"I'm just trying to say that everyone puts way too much pressure on Byron. Even the people who're supposed to be helping him. Peg never reminds him of what he's accomplished—she'd rather rag on him about how his last film didn't earn out the way it was supposed to."

Nick took a deep breath. He angled himself back in his chair and folded his arms over his chest, scowling at Miranda as he continued.

"Things haven't started out that good on this new film of his, either. The director's already been fired—the script's being rewritten while they're shooting the stupid thing. Nobody knows what anyone else is doing, and I don't think Byron should even be there yet. At least not till tempers calm down."

"Nick, if you really think Byron needs to get away, then why are you telling me? Shouldn't you be telling Byron?"

"He won't listen to me, and Peg won't let him go. Robert's the one who spirited Byron off to Italy. And it wasn't to a resort—it was a private clinic."

An ache went through Miranda's heart. "A clinic?"

"Robert arranged the whole thing and had Byron on the plane before Peg even knew about it. It was good for Byron—he's worn out, it was just what he needed. But Peg was furious when she found out."

"Does this woman run his entire life?"

"That's putting it mildly."

"Then why doesn't Robert do something about it?"

"Robert can't do anything if Byron won't let him. But Byron might listen to you. If you could tell him to take some time off—to get away by himself—"

"I can't tell him that. I don't have any *right* to tell him that—"

"He's got to get away, Miranda." Nick's voice was urgent. "It's . . . it's a matter of life and death."

Miranda stared at him. "It's not just the pressures of Byron's career, is it? You're trying to tell me something else—something—"

"Have you forgotten last night already?"

"Of course I haven't forgotten last night!"

"Byron said he heard someone call to him from the crowd. Well, not exactly from the crowd—up close to him. He said it surprised him, and he started to turn around. And the next thing he knew, Harley was falling against him, and they both landed on the ground."

"That doesn't even make sense. *Everyone* was yelling Byron's name. Why would he have turned around for just one person?"

"You know why," Nick said evenly. "You and I both know why."

Miranda lowered her eyes. She could feel Nick staring at her, could feel the tension building between them.

"He told you not to say anything, didn't he?" Nick went on. "But I already know about Starstruck. I know how Peg wants to keep this thing quiet—and I know how panicky Byron is."

Still Miranda said nothing. She sensed Nick bending close to her, felt his hand lightly upon her cheek. His fingers traced down to the tip of her chin, and he gently forced her to look up at him.

"I know how scared *you* are, too," he said solemnly.

His kiss was unexpected. Warm and soft and very sweet, yet with an unmistakable passion that sent her heart racing out of control.

"Nick," she murmured as he suddenly pulled away.

She saw him straighten in his chair, heard him swear angrily under his breath.

"There's Zena and your friends," he muttered. "They're coming this way, so we don't have much time."

"Time for what?"

She watched as he reached across the table . . . as he took her hand and squeezed it tightly in his own.

"Now there's something *you* should know," Nick whispered. "Last night . . . in the crowd . . . Byron was stabbed, too."

23

Miranda rode back in a daze.

She was thankful that everyone else was so tired from shopping—this way she didn't have to carry on a conversation with anyone. She closed her eyes and pretended to sleep, and roused again only when they'd reached the house.

She couldn't stop thinking about the talk she'd had with Nick. *Byron being stabbed . . . Nick wanting him so desperately to leave.* Her thoughts were in a whirl of confusion—she couldn't seem to sort anything out. There was so much more she wished they could have discussed, but Zena and the girls had found them, and they'd had to break off their conversation about Byron.

Nick seemed so concerned about me. . . .

Why? Miranda wondered.

Because of Starstruck? Because Nick knew that being close to Byron could put Miranda in danger?

Because Nick suspected who Starstruck really was?

The only thing Miranda knew for sure was that Starstruck was real—she *had* to be real if Nick knew about her, if Nick was so worried. She was glad he'd been so forthcoming with his information. She was glad she hadn't had to break her word to Byron about not telling anyone else.

Miranda felt as if her brain would explode. Too much was happening—too many things that made no sense. She dragged herself into the house and wished she could just fall asleep for a hundred years. As Nick unloaded the packages from the limo, he seemed about to ask her something, but before he could manage it, Peg came in with instructions for the evening.

Formal dinner in the dining room at seven o'clock. Afterward, everyone invited to the studio with Lucille and Miguel to watch a night scene being shot for Byron's new movie. Miranda scarcely listened to Peg's announcement. At one time she would have been overjoyed at the prospect of seeing a film being made—but now it seemed almost anticlimactic with everything else she'd been through. The others disappeared out onto the terrace for hors d'oeuvres. Miranda started upstairs, when Peg stopped her.

"Miranda," she said, "if you don't mind, I'd like to talk to you about something after dinner."

Miranda hesitated. "About what?"

"I'd rather not say here," Peg replied. "Suppose I come to your room later on?"

Miranda couldn't help but be curious. She paused, then nodded stiffly in Peg's direction. "That'd be fine."

"Nothing formal, just a comfortable, relaxing little talk. Just you and me."

"All right. See you then."

Mystified, Miranda went on to her room. After showering and changing clothes, she rejoined the others by the pool, then made a halfhearted attempt at dinner. Peg had a previous commitment, she was told, and wouldn't be there till later, but the rest of the group seemed to have made it. She begged off from the studio visit, despite Jo's urgent pleadings, and stood at the front door waving as Nick took them away in the limo. She didn't know where Robert had disappeared to, or Zena. The kitchen staff had also vanished, and she supposed the rest of the household had settled down to some leisurely evening time.

She glanced at the clock as she went upstairs. It was just a little after ten, but the house was as still as midnight. For a brief second she wished Jo and Kelly were back here again, just for the sound of their voices. Her feet were literally dragging, she was so tired. The hall to her room seemed unusually long tonight . . . unnaturally quiet.

She stifled a yawn as she walked. She'd gotten about halfway down the corridor when she heard something behind her and whirled around.

The hallway was empty.

Still . . . Miranda could have *sworn* she heard something back there. The sound of a door closing, perhaps?

She narrowed her eyes, scanning both sides of the passageway. Had all the doors been shut before? She thought so, but she couldn't be sure.

She frowned and continued on. There were lights high up along the walls, and they seemed to flicker a little as she passed them. Almost as though the power was failing . . . or maybe the bulbs were burning out. Had they always done that when she'd gone by? Miranda couldn't remember.

She walked faster. She reached her room and put her hand on the doorknob, stopping just a second to glance back over her shoulder. The hall flickered softly, half light, half shadow. There wasn't a sound now. Not a whisper.

She hurried inside and locked the door behind her. She leaned back against it and put a hand to her heart, forcing herself to be calm. *What's the matter with you, you're acting so silly!* Peg would be here any minute—she certainly didn't want to be flustered when that horrible woman arrived. But . . . what was that strange noise?

Miranda stiffened and strained her ears. It sounded as if someone had left the water on in the bathroom, or the shower hadn't been turned off. Cautiously she flicked on the bathroom light. All the taps were off, securely in place—yet she could still hear water running.

She stood uncertainly by the closet, letting her eyes travel slowly around the room. Her bed had been turned down, the usual chocolate mints left on her pillow. She went over and picked up the telephone. She'd call one of the staff and report the noise and have someone come up to check it out. If something was leaking, they'd surely want to know about it.

Miranda held the receiver to her ear, and then she frowned. There was no dial tone. The phone was dead.

That's weird. . . . Guess I should tell someone about that, too.

She put the phone back down and stepped away, glancing over at the French doors. They were standing open just a little, and that's when she began to realize that the water sound was coming from outside.

Miranda began walking toward the balcony. She slowly opened the doors and peered out into the darkness.

A scream rose into her throat. From the dim light of the bedroom, she could see someone sitting there in the hot tub. Someone whose back was to her, showing just a silhouette of head and shoulders. Someone relaxing in the rushing water.

"Peg!" Miranda exclaimed.

She felt weak with relief. Laughing nervously, she marched out onto the balcony.

"Peg, you scared me to death! I didn't know you were out here!" Moving closer, Miranda added, "When you said a relaxing talk, I didn't know you meant—"

And then she broke off.

She stopped behind Peg, and she stared.

Peg wasn't answering, nor was she turning around.

In fact, she just continued to sit there, gazing off into the darkness, not uttering a word.

"Peg?" Miranda said again. "Peg, what's wrong?"

She put one hand on Peg's shoulder.

For a split second Peg tilted sideways. And then she slid swiftly beneath the water.

Miranda stared in horror. She could see the water churning, churning, the frothy red bubbles, and the knife stuck there through Peg's heart.

"Peg!"

Miranda screamed. She screamed Peg's name, but before she could turn around, something came down on the back of her head—something that hit with a soft, dull thud—something that swirled her into a vast, empty silence.

24

Everything was black.

As Miranda's eyes slowly opened, she wondered if she was dreaming—only *dreaming* that she was opening her eyes, for no matter which way she tried to look, there was only darkness.

The pain hit from out of nowhere.

It hit her hard and throbbing, and with a gasp she tried to lift her hand to the back of her head. Her arm weighed a ton; her brain felt thick and sluggish. When she finally managed to touch her hair, her fingertips felt damp and sticky.

I'm bleeding. I'm bleeding . . . and I don't know where I am. . . .

And then she began to remember.

Slowly, hazily, it all started coming back to her. Walking out to the balcony of her room . . . Peg's lifeless body sinking into the hot tub . . . The sudden crush on the back of her skull . . .

But where am I now?

Terror surged through her. She realized she was lying down, lying on her stomach, and she groped out tentatively with one hand. There was a hard surface beneath her, and her fingers trailed in dust. She could hear water, but not the hot tub anymore—this was more like . . .

Rain?

Yes, rain—she could *smell* it now, too. Rain and sawdust and cedar . . .

From some distant memory Miranda realized that she'd smelled these things before, and not so very long ago.

Moaning softly, she tried to sit up. The darkness whirled around her, and she grabbed her head between her hands. After a while she pulled herself into a sitting position. . . . After a while she sniffed the air once more.

Byron's cabin.

Miranda stared silently into the blackness. The stark terror she'd felt only seconds before was fading now. Strangely enough, she didn't feel any emotion at all.

What am I doing in Byron's cabin?

She thought she heard someone whispering. A cautious voice that seemed very far away. "Byron?" it called. "Byron, are you there?" And then she realized it was *her* voice she was hearing—her own voice floating back to her, as eerie as the emptiness around her.

A burst of thunder shuddered the floor. She lay

down flat upon it, pressed both palms against the floorboards, against the wild, resonant trembling of the storm. Dust clung to her fingertips, thickened with smears of her own blood.

I'm the next victim, she realized.

I'm the next victim, and I'm going to die.

And how strange, she thought vaguely, that this should be happening to her, just because she won a contest, just because she won a dream come true. . . .

But this isn't a dream.

And I've got to get out of here.

Reason began to take over, and with it a calm sense of survival. She couldn't just lie here and wait for whatever might happen. She tried to sit up again, but the darkness spun sickeningly on every side. Very slowly she began to crawl.

She wasn't exactly sure of her location, but something told her she must be in the main room of the cabin. As her eyes carefully probed the dark, she was finally able to make out just the faintest difference in shadows, and she realized it was a window space in the wall. She lifted her head higher and stared. Yes, she could see it now—the paler darkness of the sky beyond . . . a faint thread of faraway lightning.

She tried to remember. She tried to remember where the door was . . . which direction to move. She tried to think of that and nothing more.

Her head ached terribly. It was as if night were flowing back and forth, back and forth, between the cabin and her brain. She told herself she had to stand up. She told herself she had to stand, that she couldn't pass out, no matter what. She gritted her teeth and willed her body upright. She choked down a wave of nausea and stretched out her hands and groped through the hollow endlessness.

The air was cool beneath her fingers. Cool with just the faintest ripple of movement. Almost as though it had been stirred by someone breathing . . . the whisper of an invisible breath . . .

Her hands brushed across a face.

Screaming, Miranda fell back. She crouched on the floor and thrashed out wildly with her arms, fighting the empty dark. Nothing was there. Only the sound of her own terror, only the struggle of her own fear . . .

I must have imagined it.

She fought back tears and braced herself against a rush of raging pain. *I'm all disoriented—I'm imagining things that aren't there—*

She forced herself to calm down. Once more she reached out her hands. She stood up. She took a step. When something rustled off to her side, she instinctively spun toward it, and felt the warmth of human skin.

"Who's there!" she screamed. *"Who are you!"*

But whatever she'd touched had vanished.

"You know how it is when you feel someone watching you—when you feel eyes staring at the back of your head. . . ."

As Byron's words came back to her, Miranda froze where she stood. For she knew without a doubt that *someone* was there—that someone *was* watching her—she could *feel* it—could feel the power and disdain, could feel the cold amusement, even as she cowered there like a frightened animal in a trap. . . .

"Who *are* you!" she cried again. "What do you want!"

And then the voice . . . soft and deep and whispery . . . behind her in the darkness where she couldn't see . . .

"I'm Starstruck," it whispered. "And you're dead."

And she could hear movement now, too—footsteps slow and steady, creaking on the floorboards, circling all around her—

Stay calm, Miranda—for God's sake, stay calm!

"What have I done to you?" Miranda forced her voice under control—fought to keep it steady. "Tell me what I've done, and we'll talk. Maybe I can help you."

There was no answer. The footsteps seemed to have stopped. The air was still.

"Are you here?" Miranda whispered. "Why don't you tell me what's—"

A light burst on, blinding her.

Instinctively Miranda put up her arms to shield her eyes from the glare. For several moments she couldn't see anything at all, but then, as her arms began to lower, she squinted in the direction of the flashlight.

She could see something now . . .

Someone now.

A tall, dark figure slowly materializing from a doorway . . .

Someone she knew . . .

"Oh, God," she whispered. "Nick."

"Come to me, Miranda," Nick said quietly. "Come to me now."

"No, Miranda," another voice spoke behind her. "Come to *me.*"

Shocked, Miranda whirled around.

From the glow of a lantern she could see yet another human shadow forming, framed there in yet another doorway. . . .

Miranda stared, her eyes going wide.

"Byron!" she gasped.

25

Miranda." Slowly Byron reached out for her. "Be careful . . . just move this way—"

"Don't do it!" Nick shouted. "He'll kill you if you do!"

Byron's arm lowered again to his side. "You can't believe anything Nick says. He's trying to turn you against me. He's been trying to all along."

"He's the one lying! He made it all up—all that stuff about Starstruck—he made up *everything!*"

Miranda stood there frozen. As she looked wildly from one to the other, she suddenly realized that both Nick and Byron were clutching guns in their hands.

"Byron . . . you're supposed to be in the hospital," Miranda murmured. "You were stabbed—you—"

"He did that himself." Nick hesitated, his voice

going hard. "He faked the whole thing. He killed Harley, too, just to make it look like some crazy fan. And then he walked out of the hospital tonight—"

"Right, Miranda, listen to Nick. I killed my own bodyguard. And then I stabbed myself! I guess I'll do anything to get attention!"

"He left the hospital, don't you get it?"

"I left for a reason! Because it suddenly *hit* me while I was lying in that hospital bed! How Starstruck's voice had sounded so familiar to me on the phone, even though I could tell it was disguised! How it almost sounded like someone I remembered—someone I *knew!* Like all those character voices Nick used to use in our drama class. He was always so good at voices—always so good at pretending to be someone else—"

"He's lying, Miranda—he left the hospital tonight to kill *you*. He killed Peg, and now he needs *you* to play it out! There never was a Starstruck. He did it for the publicity—so everyone would feel sorry for him and sympathetic—but Peg wouldn't buy it! So he had to kill her to get her out of the way! And now you'll be Starstruck's last victim!"

"Does that make sense? My face is known all over the world—do I *need* that kind of negative publicity?"

"I can see the headlines now—'Byron Slater's girlfriend struck down by possessive fan'! Did you really think you'd get *away* with this?"

"Did *you*, Nick?"

Silence stretched out, cold and tense.

At last Nick spoke again, his voice softening.

"Your last film was a big disappointment, wasn't

it, Byron. The studio's been putting pressure on you—*everyone's* been putting pressure on you! You're afraid you're on your way down—that some new star will pass you by. This whole Starstruck thing was just a stunt to keep the media attention focused on you. Poor Byron—stalked and terrorized by some heartsick fan—"

"God, you're good, Nick—you've almost managed to convince *me!* Maybe those acting lessons weren't such a waste of time, after all."

"Stop it!" Miranda cried. "Stop it, both of you!"

"But we want to know the truth, don't we?" Byron insisted. "We want to know the real reason why Nick killed Peg. Because she got *my* career started, that's why. Because she got *me* that lead part instead of Nick. She was working for a big director, and she had an in. And Nick always swore he'd get even with her, because she handed *me* that break and not him. Don't you see, he's been biding his time? And tonight when Peg called and said she was so scared—"

"Peg never called him!"

"She *called* me. Harley's family's been asking a lot of questions, and she was afraid the press was going to find out he'd been stabbed. She was afraid someone *else* might be killed."

"And I guess she had good reason to be afraid, didn't she."

Miranda's eyes blurred with tears. Her head was pounding—pounding—

"Miranda, listen to me," Nick went on urgently. "It was *Robert* who asked me to come and work here. He was worried about Byron—he said he hadn't been acting like himself, and he wanted me to help keep an eye on him. I was supposed to try and convince him to go away for a while. Robert wanted to put him in a private clinic in Switzerland—get him some help—"

"I'm not the one who needs help," Byron interrupted. "You made the phone calls, and you smuggled the book into my study. You let Simba out of her cage. You tampered with the car that morning, too. And you came up behind me in the crowd outside the club. Everyone thought you were in the limo, but you didn't get there till later. You came up behind me, and then you killed Harley, and then you tried to kill me, too. I know, because I saw you in the crowd."

"Then how'd I get back to the limo so fast? Everyone saw me there—*all* of them saw me there. You'll have to do better than that!"

"You've been getting rid of every single person who means anything to me, Nick," Byron said sadly. "You've tried to ruin my success by making everyone think I'm crazy. You got rid of Harley, and you got rid of Peg. And now—because you know how I feel about Miranda—you've been trying to get rid of her, too. You knew about that broken statue by the pool—you followed us up to the cabin and did a job on my car that morning—"

"There was nothing wrong with the car. I checked it out that morning."

"But I was there!" Miranda burst out. "The car *did* go out of control! Something really *was* wrong with it!"

"Think, Miranda, think!" Nick pleaded. "He does

his own stunts! He only wanted you to believe that something was wrong!"

"He put the heart in your room," Byron fired back.

"What heart? I don't know what you're talking about!"

"He knew everyone else would be gone tonight. He knew you and Peg would be there alone. He cut the phone lines so you couldn't call for help—"

"He cut them himself!" Nick's voice rose in desperation. "So the hospital couldn't call and tell you he'd walked out! For God's sake, Miranda, if you don't trust *me,* then run! *Run!* Don't let him find you!"

"Bad idea," Byron said softly. "I'll kill you before you get to the door."

Miranda stared at him.

He was smiling, and his gun was aimed at her heart.

From some faraway place, she thought she heard a clicking sound. Tears streamed down her face.

"It's over, Byron," Nick said softly. "You can't kill both of us. Just put the gun down, and let me help you."

"Put the gun down?" Byron gave a harsh laugh. "I'm a hero, Nick. Heroes never put their guns down. Heroes go out in magnificent blazes of glory."

"Byron, please." Nick's voice lowered even more. Miranda could see his outstretched hand, could see the nozzle of his gun gleaming there in the light. The bullet would go straight through Byron's forehead, directly between his eyes. Nick's hand wasn't even shaking.

"Let Miranda go," Nick tried again. "She doesn't have anything to do with this."

Again the endless silence.

Miranda could feel her heart racing, the pounding of terror through her veins.

And then Byron started to laugh.

He started to laugh, and he started to clap, and his gun swayed from side to side.

"Really touching, Nick. And so heartfelt! Why, I almost believe you *want* to help me. I almost believe you *can* act!"

"Leave, Miranda," Nick whispered. His eyes never moved from Byron's face. "Leave while you still can."

Miranda was never sure what happened next.

As an explosion of gunfire ricocheted through the cabin, the lights went out and she ran for the door. She didn't even realize she was outside until she stumbled and fell, sprawling full-length upon the wet, muddy ground.

Rain washed down in torrents.

Thunder heaved the murky clouds, and lightning split the sky.

Sobbing, she struggled to her feet. Her whole body shrieked with pain. As the sky burst white above her, she spotted the Land Rover only several yards away. She jumped inside, but the keys were gone. Frantically she searched for a car phone, but before she could get it to work, a gun fired right behind her and she raced away.

The road—where was the road! She ran toward where she remembered, toward where she thought it must be. She ran ankle-deep in mud, slipping and sliding and staggering up again. She ran as far as she could, then realized too late that she'd come to the edge of a cliff.

There was no place left to go.

She could hear footsteps behind her—*pounding* behind her—closer and closer. In sheer panic she swung back around to face her pursuer and felt her foot turn sideways, felt the wet ground crumbling beneath her shoe.

She slipped to the edge of the cliff. Her hands grabbed frantically for a hold, and her scream echoed on and on through the rainy night.

"Oh, God," Miranda sobbed. "I'm really going to fall!"

She dangled high above the sheer drop. Her whole face seemed frozen, a mask of horror and stunned resignation as she prepared to plunge to her death.

"Miranda!" a voice shouted. "Miranda, where are you!"

She tried to answer. She opened her mouth and screamed again, but the thunder drowned out her cries. She could feel the earth melting away beneath her fingertips. . . . She could feel chunks of it running down her arms, spattering down her legs.

"Oh, God, help me!" she sobbed.

"Miranda!"

Lightning exploded above her. For one split second she saw a face silhouetted against the raging sky.

"Give me your hand!" Nick shouted.

"I can't! I'll fall!"

"No, you won't! Just give me your hand!"

She saw him reach out. She saw his hand close tightly over hers . . . felt her fingers pulling loose from the mud.

Nick had ahold of her wrist.

And then he let go.

Miranda shrieked in terror. The night sky tilted crazily overhead as she clawed for something to hold on to. Rocks came loose in her hands—the whole mountainside seemed to be melting beneath her. With one last surge of strength, she grabbed at a dangling tree root, then hung there for dear life.

"Miranda!"

She was afraid to look up. She was afraid to move, to even breathe. Rain lashed her mercilessly, and a terrible coldness numbed her all the way through.

This is it. I really am going to die.

She closed her eyes, then opened them again. She peered up at the ledge and saw Nick's face framed there against the storm.

One second he was looking down at her.

The next instant Byron loomed behind him and shoved him toward the edge.

"Nick!" Miranda screamed.

She saw him fighting desperately, his feet struggling for a hold, his body twisting and turning, trying to balance on the rocks.

She saw him slide halfway over the edge.

"Nick! No!"

Miranda screamed again. She saw Nick's hand shoot out and close around Byron's ankle—that split second of surprise on Byron's face as lightning burst overhead and his feet went helplessly out from under him. . . .

He fell sideways. Just as Nick managed to drag himself up again and give Byron one final push.

Miranda heard the cry.

A cry of rage and horrified anguish.

And then he was falling . . .

Falling silently past her to the endless dark below.

26

Miranda stared out the airplane window.

The California landscape grew smaller and smaller as the plane climbed high into the clouds.

Sunshine.

Bright, pure wonderful light, warm and clean and . . . real.

I'm going home, she thought wearily. *Home.*

She felt as if she'd been gone for years and years, not just a matter of days. She glanced over at the seat beside her, at the tray in its down position, at the newspaper spread out flat upon it.

CELEBRITY SCANDAL, the headline read. MURDER AND SUICIDE MORE DRAMATIC THAN ANY FILM.

Miranda sighed and closed her eyes. She didn't need to read the article; she already knew what it said. How Byron Slater, severely depressed since his last film, had suffered a mental breakdown. How

Byron Slater had murdered his publicist during an argument, then fled to his mountain cabin in a raging storm. How Byron Slater, desperate and filled with remorse, had taken his own life by throwing himself off a cliff. . . .

Yes, she already knew what the article said about Byron Slater; she'd already read it at least a dozen times. It talked about how worried everyone had been, how even a respite in Italy had failed to cheer him up, how he'd been suffering delusions and paranoia and extreme fits of moodiness. . . .

Miranda closed her eyes.

Tears stung behind her eyelids, and again she remembered.

How she and Nick had finally made it home that night. How one of the maids had discovered Peg's body in their absence and called for help. The house had been crawling with police, but Nick had simply driven past the gates, then sneaked in the back way to the estate. They'd gone straight to his apartment to clean up and change clothes. And by the time the others returned from their visit to the studio, no one even noticed when she and Nick finally made their appearance in the midst of all the confusion.

She remembered the stricken look on Robert's face. How he'd sat there staring, lost in his private grief. Lucille stunned, Jo and Kelly crying. And Zena, mumbling over and over again about how *perfect* Byron was, how perfect Byron's *life* was. "He had *everything,*" she'd kept insisting, "everything to live for . . . everything anyone could ever want. . . ."

They'd taken a vow of silence, she and Nick. And it was strange, Miranda thought now, how it had never even been mentioned between them, how somehow it had seemed completely understood, the only right thing they could possibly do.

For Byron.

They'd just told everyone they'd gone out together for a drive, and no one had any reason to doubt them. After all, Nick was only the hired help. And Miranda was only one of three lucky contest winners who'd gone there for a dream come true. . . .

Dream come true . . .

Miranda smiled sadly to herself. There'd be no chance at stardom for any of them now. No more female roles to fill in any more Byron Slater movies . . .

"Miranda . . . you okay?"

Miranda opened her eyes. She turned her head to the seat next to her.

"I'm okay." She smiled. "Really."

"Well, I was just thinking again."

"You know how dangerous that is. In fact, I don't even know why you risk it."

Nick grinned. "You sure your folks won't mind my coming home with you? I feel sort of weird just dropping in like this."

"Why would they mind? You *did* save my life, you know. They wanted to meet you in person."

"Maybe I'm not quite what they're expecting."

Miranda did a quick appraisal of his jeans, red sneakers, and orange shirt. She hid a smile. "Well, if we're *really* lucky, maybe your suitcase will end up in the Great Beyond like mine did."

"Okay, so I'm not a *GQ* kind of guy. But I *am* a pretty nice view."

Miranda's mouth fell open. "Nick! You weren't supposed to hear that!"

"Yeah. I knew that first day at the airport that you were really hot for me."

She laughed then. She looked into Nick's mischievous blue eyes and saw his hand reach out and gently take hers.

"Just remember," he said quietly. "I'm no Byron Slater, okay?"

Miranda fixed him with a solemn stare. "I don't want a Byron Slater. And you know something . . . I don't think I *ever* did."

Nick grinned. He leaned over and touched her gently on the cheek.

And then he kissed her.

Real, Miranda thought. *Real and sincere and genuine, just like Nick.*

Just perfect.

About the Author

Richie Tankersley Cusick loves to read and write scary books. Richie enjoys writing when it is rainy and gloomy outside, and likes to have a spooky soundtrack playing in the background. She writes at a desk that originally belonged to a funeral director in the 1800s and that she believes is haunted. Halloween is one of her favorite holidays. She decorates the entire house, which includes having a body laid out in state in the parlor, life-size models of Frankenstein's monster, the figure of Death to keep watch, and scary costumes for Hannah and Meg, her dogs. A neighbor told her that a previous owner of the house was feared by all of the neighborhood kids and no one would go to the house on Halloween.

Richie is the author of *Vampire, Fatal Secrets, The Locker, The Mall, Silent Stalker, Help Wanted, The Drifter, Someone at the Door, Summer of Secrets, Overdue,* and the novelization of *Buffy the Vampire Slayer,* in addition to several adult novels for Pocket Books. She lives outside Kansas City, where she is currently at work on her next novel.